"I'll do my best to keep this killer away
from you, Lindsey. I promise."

"I believe you. Still, you hardly know me." She tilted

side

her

bath,

ss

ers

g on

aving

st time

ted at

She stood there with her mouth open at the audacity
of his words. *Our first time?*

her face to look at him.

"Then that's something we'll have to change."

Brian delivered a trail of hot kisses down the ... of her face and continued a path back up to ... forehead. Lindsay turned her mouth into his ... and the fireworks were as explosive as the ki... earlier that morning.

Their tongues danced and explored. His fing... barely grazed her waist and then she felt a t... both sides of her shirt. Brian backed away, le... her lips cold and desperate for more of him.

"As much as I'd like to keep on with this—" he ... dropped another kiss on her cheek "—but th... is not going to be what we could be interrupt... any moment."

THE RENEGADE RANCHER

ANGI MORGAN

HARLEQUIN®INTRIGUE®

Recycling programs for this product may not exist in your area.

Many moons ago, I graduated from high school with a small group of kids. Brian & Johnny are fictional characters, but named after two men who won't be returning at our next reunion. I have used the names of people in my hometown, but not their personalities. The characters are fictional, but not my friendships or the respect I have for the namesakes.

ISBN-13: 978-0-373-69766-3

THE RENEGADE RANCHER

Copyright © 2014 by Angela Platt

All rights reserved. Except for use in any review, the reproduction or utilization of this work in whole or in part in any form by any electronic, mechanical or other means, now known or hereafter invented, including xerography, photocopying and recording, or in any information storage or retrieval system, is forbidden without the written permission of the publisher, Harlequin Enterprises Limited, 225 Duncan Mill Road, Don Mills, Ontario M3B 3K9, Canada.

This is a work of fiction. Names, characters, places and incidents are either the product of the author's imagination or are used fictitiously, and any resemblance to actual persons, living or dead, business establishments, events or locales is entirely coincidental.

This edition published by arrangement with Harlequin Books S.A.

For questions and comments about the quality of this book, please contact us at CustomerService@Harlequin.com.

® and TM are trademarks of Harlequin Enterprises Limited or its corporate affiliates. Trademarks indicated with ® are registered in the United States Patent and Trademark Office, the Canadian Trade Marks Office and in other countries.

www.Harlequin.com

Printed in U.S.A.

ABOUT THE AUTHOR

Angi Morgan writes Harlequin Intrigue novels "where honor and danger collide with love." She combines actual Texas settings with characters who are in realistic and dangerous situations. Angi has been a finalist for the Booksellers' Best Award, *RT Book Reviews* Best First Series, Gayle Wilson Award of Excellence and the Daphne du Maurier Award.

Angi and her husband live in north Texas, with only the four-legged "kids" left in the house to interrupt her writing. They recently began volunteering for a local Labrador foster program. Visit her website, www.angimorgan.com, or hang out with her on Facebook.

Books by Angi Morgan

CAST OF CHARACTERS

Brian Sloane—He recently discovered that he and his twin were framed for a fire that covered up a possible murder that set him on a very lonely road. He's determined to clear his name and save the girl... no matter the cost.

Lindsey Cook—Plagued with guilt over her cousin's death, she's living a life that's not her own. She thinks Brian is a little crazy when he tells her someone's been killing her family members under the guise of accidents. Can she believe the cowboy paramedic? Or will the murderer succeed in his quest?

John Sloane—Brian's identical twin and a recently retired navy SEAL. He's helping with the ranch and discouraging Brian's investigation in order to protect his new family.

J. W. Sloane—Widower, owner of the Double Bar Ranch and father to the twins. He's about to lose his property and is still recovering from a major stroke.

Mabel Standridge—Owns a house next to the Sloanes' Double Bar Ranch and helps the brothers with the care of J.W.

Jeremy Cook—Lindsey's cousin and only relative until he drowned in a devastating snorkeling accident in Cozumel. Or was it murder, as Brian claims?

Gillian Cook—Died of injuries from a tragic barn fire twelve years ago. Brian took the blame for her death to protect his brother. They recently discovered someone framed them for the accident. Does that make it murder?

Chapter One

Tall, blond and deadly gorgeous.

Brian Sloane knew that Lindsey Cook was a looker. One glance would let any male with eyes know that fact. Platinum blond hair that hung to her waist, classic blue eyes that would disappear next to a clear summer sky and a body that should be gracing covers of magazines. A looker, all right.

This was the longest he'd ever been with a woman and he hadn't met her yet.

He knew how old she was, where she'd graduated from college, that her best friend's name was Beth. All that information was on her internet site. He knew she lived in Arlington, drove a sports car, kept two goldfish and was allergic to cats. She'd had five jobs in the past three years and did freelance web design. He also knew why she'd migrated to Texas after burying her cousin. Jeremy had drowned while they'd been on vacation together about six months ago and she'd stayed after settling his affairs. Her cousin's *female* lawyer had been extrachatty during happy hour.

Unfortunately, accidents happened everywhere, leaving one question he couldn't answer. How long she would live.

Brian entered the sandwich shop and tried not to zoom

all his attention on her. Searching the remaining tables, he noticed no one else was alone, so it was probably safe to assume she was his appointment. "Lindsey?"

"You're Brian?" she asked, extending her hand. Her smile could mesmerize him. He'd watched her work that magic on several customers—male and female—over the past couple of weeks.

"That'd be me." He took a slender palm in his own, gave a quick squeeze and sat at the table. A well-chosen table in the middle of the very empty sandwich shop. The red silky blouse clung everywhere and plunged just enough to make his imagination go a little wild.

"So, you said that Jeremy's lawyer recommended me for a job. Your email said something about a ranch website?"

"Yeah, about that. This might sound strange, but I've been doing some research and—" Was that sudden look in her eyes one of surprise? An alert? How had he messed up?

"No website?"

He stared, thinking hard on what his answer should be. It was important she listen to him. Her life depended on it. He couldn't just say that. Could he? He'd avoided the truth long enough. "To be honest—"

"Excuse me just a sec." She looked into her purse. She brought her keys to the tabletop. Hooked to the ring— now pointed at his face—was a small can of pepper spray. "Who are you and why have you been following me? I saw you in front of the store yesterday and you were in line behind me when I got coffee last week."

"Whoa there." He raised his hands, trying not to jump away from that can. "I really am Brian Sloane. I'm a Fort Worth paramedic, just like I said on the phone. I've got ID."

She shook her head slowly from side to side. Was she thinking about believing him or shooting that pepper spray into his eyes? Okay, so he'd slipped up and not only let her see him a couple of times, but he'd made eye contact at the coffee shop. Who could have resisted? She was smoking hot.

"I'm going to leave," she said, "and you'd better stop following me. Just so you know, I took your picture when you walked in and if I see you again—even by accident— I'll report you to the police as a stalker."

He leaned forward, and she jerked to attention. *Skittish as a newborn colt.* "I know this is a weird way to meet."

"To say the least." She kept the nozzle pointed at his eyes. Extremely close to his eyes.

"But I do have information regarding your family."

"I don't have any family."

"What I mean is…I've been doing research and I think Jeremy was murdered."

"I thought you were an EMT. You sound like a reporter." She brought her finely shaped eyebrows into a straight line, showing her scrutiny and distrust. Not knowing she'd just delivered an insult to highly trained paramedics everywhere by calling him an entry-level EMT.

With a new sister-in-law around his house, he was picking up on a lot of subtle feminine looks that he'd had no clue about before. This look? Well, it didn't leave any room for interpretation.

He shifted. She jerked.

"Just getting my wallet. Okay?"

"Is there a problem, Lindsey?" The guy behind the sandwich counter stopped wiping the display cases.

"I'm fine. Just dealing with another jerk reporter."

"I'm not a reporter." He shook his head, looked at the

big fellow who was very defensive of the woman in front of him and repeated, "I'm *not* a reporter."

"Then why are you following me?"

"It's a long story and I'd rather not have pepper spray aimed at me while I tell it."

Lindsey's long, straight hair gently framed a delicate, expressive, beautiful face that he'd been attracted to since the first picture he'd seen of her online. It sort of took him by surprise when she leaned back in her chair, dropped her hands to her lap and waited, the key ring in plain sight. Her protector returned to cleaning. The shop's patrons went back to business as usual.

"I'd like the short version, please," she said, pushing her hair behind her ear. "You've got five minutes and then I'm leaving."

Short? How did he explain such a complicated story?

"All right. Twelve years ago I thought my brother caused the accidental fire that took the life of one of our former teachers, your second cousin, Gillian Cook. But I was wrong. She was murdered."

"Take it to the police." She pushed back her chair and scooped her keys into her purse, clearly taking off.

"You said I had five minutes."

She stood. Her long hair swayed at her waist, drawing his attention to the fraction of flat belly he could see above her jeans when her shirt rose up as she took a deep breath.

"You have five seconds to remove your hand from my arm or I'll let Craig—" she tipped her head to the sandwich guy, who threw down his bar towel "—deal with you. Four. Three."

Craig dashed to the end of the counter. Brian dropped his hold. Lindsey stared at him as her friend reached for his shirt. He'd been so caught up in her leaving that he hadn't realized he'd grabbed her arm to stop her.

"Sorry. I didn't mean to scare you."

"Wait. Craig, wait." She waved off the man's attempt to lift Brian from the chair—*through* the table. "Look, I'm very tired of people hounding me about my accident-prone family. There have been terrible emails from someone thinking I'm a jinx." She hid her eyes behind slender fingers, then shoved her hair behind her ear again and straightened her back. "I know what happened to my family. I live with it every day, and to have it in the paper or on a blog is disrespectful. It's mean and I've had enough. Just leave me alone."

She tilted her face toward her chest, hiding behind her hair.

"Your family didn't do anything wrong." Brilliant blue eyes opened wide to search him. Why was she ashamed? "Besides, I don't think they were accidents. And I'm fairly certain you're next."

"Seriously? You think someone's out to kill me?" Her long nails were the exact color of one of the flowers on her shirt. It was easy to see with her hand nervously rubbing her collarbone.

"I haven't been stalking you, Miss Cook. Our paths crossed while I was looking into your cousin's life," he explained. It was true enough. He had been looking into Jeremy Cook.

Craig stood guard at her shoulder, ready to do battle, his arms crossed over a massive chest. It was plain why Lindsey had chosen this location to meet a stranger. "Take it to the cops," Craig said. "You ready for me to throw this jerk out?"

One cross look would have Brian's face pulverized before he could defend himself. Well, Craig could try.

Brian had fought with the best around his hometown
for a long time. So he shrugged. He'd never convince
her while including muscleman in the conversation. She
didn't believe him. Hell, he hardly believed himself. His
theory was so far out there he hadn't even shared it with
his family.

He'd tried, right? That was all he could do. He pressed
on the table to push his chair back and long, bright nails
tapped quickly near his hand, gaining his attention.

"It's okay, Craig. I'm okay." She looked up at her protector and winked at him, immediately relaxing the big
guy and getting her way.

Brian waited until they were alone and lowered his
voice, leaning closer across the table. "Look, I'm not a
cop or a detective or a reporter. I really am just a horse
rancher who pays the bills by working as a paramedic."

"You're wowing me with so many reasons to believe
you." She laughed. Her eyes sparkled and were sad at
the same time.

He understood that. How an enjoyable moment could
catch you off guard and you forget—just for an instant.
Then the reason you don't laugh comes rushing back to
blur the happy. Yeah, he understood.

"You have every right to wonder about my motives.
You should be careful. I should have left this info with
your lawyer and never bothered you in person. I'll be
on my way."

"Why did you? Come here, that is."

The tap on the tabletop drew his eyes back to her
hands, then up her tanned arms, to her shoulders and
neck. The slow tap and arch of her eyebrow showed him
she knew he'd been taking a long look. He expected a
wink any second, and would probably do whatever she
asked. He was *that* attracted.

He pushed himself straighter in the chair and caught her doing a little looking of her own.

"I can't convince you to trust me. I'll drop everything off at your lawyer's office after I get out of your hair."

"Wait. I, um… If you're really not a reporter, can you begin again? Take five more minutes?" She brought part of her hair in front of her shoulder and began twisting strands into a tiny braid. "Start with what the police said."

"That I was crazy."

"I can't imagine why." She smiled, sliding back into the chair next to him. "I'm sorry and really trying to understand why you think someone's trying to kill me. You have to admit, it's not news you get every day."

He'd give her that point. He also liked her sassiness. "When you look at each family, the deaths seem to be open-and-shut accidents. But a friend of mine who's big on genealogy did a search. And then there's the regular intervals of the accidents. My brother caught that when—"

"Why do you think I'm next?" she interrupted, eyes worried, her breathing rapid.

"You're the only one left."

Chapter Two

Lindsey wanted to run from the shop and the memories. But the man leaning across the table looking so concerned on her behalf intrigued her. She still had doubts and couldn't possibly believe his theory. It didn't hurt to hear him out. She glanced at the clock behind him. She had plenty of time before she needed to be at work.

His hand covered hers. "I'm really sorry. I shouldn't have said it like that. I'm not used to this kind of conversation."

She could feel the calluses, the warmth, the strength. He looked genuinely worried. A shiver crept up her back. The eerie kind that could make you look under your bed after watching a shark movie. But that was nonsense, just like thinking all her family had been murdered.

"When Jeremy died, I made the mistake of mentioning to one of his friends that he was my last close relative. He didn't wait until Jeremy had been buried before he blogged about the accidents of those close to me. He ranted about how *lucky* I seemed to escape death while those close to me didn't and insinuated there may be foul play."

"That's why you thought I was a reporter. I don't blame you for grabbing your pepper spray."

Brian Sloane wasn't anything like she'd expected.

Honestly, she'd thought the man following her would be a psychopath. Someone following her for a really weird reason like they loved her nails or something. So if this tall cowboy wasn't following her and hadn't been the one asking Craig questions earlier this week, then who was the mystery man and how would she find him?

"Why do *you* think someone wants to kill me, Mr. Sloane?"

"Brian, please. My daddy's still Mr. Sloane and is the only one who deserves that title."

A good-looking cowboy who could charm his way anywhere, she'd bet. It was easy to see the solid, chiseled body just under his T-shirt. Hard not to imagine the strength that came with the square jaw and high cheekbones. *Not so fast, Mr. Sloane.*

"We haven't found a reason."

"We? I thought the police didn't believe you."

"A neighbor and my sister-in-law have been helping me." He leaned his chiseled jaw on his elbow. "Discovering the truth is important to my family. Everybody's chipped in some research time."

"Maybe you should start at the beginning?" And maybe she shouldn't look too much at that million-dollar smile.

"Four months ago, I began trying to find the family of a neighbor and teacher in Aubrey—the town where I live. She died just after my high school graduation in an accident I was blamed for."

"A second cousin who I never met."

He nodded. "I started looking just after Jeremy drowned in Cozumel. His death made the news in Fort Worth, so I recognized his name."

"He was snorkeling. His body had lots of small cuts and scratches. They think he got caught in the coral." She relived Jeremy's drowning almost every night and hoped to forgive herself one day. "Over forty people were in the water and no one saw anything."

His grip on her hand tightened and he nodded as if he understood.

"Mabel, my dad's friend, researched your family tree. Every name she gave me passed from an accident." He paused and removed a piece of paper from his back pocket. "Here. Fourteen names. They're all related to you and all died in the past twenty years. Most out of state."

He pushed the paper over to her with a long finger, then leaned back in his chair, lacing those fingers together behind his neck. His brows arched high, waiting for her to acknowledge his assumptions.

"The police are right. A list doesn't prove anything."

"Don't you see?" He jumped forward, his hand landing a little too loudly on the tabletop.

Lindsey automatically reached for the mace again, stopping herself when she saw the concern in Brian's puppy-brown eyes. Wouldn't it be the perfect ploy for a serial killer to pose as the person trying to stop himself?

Don't be a ninny.

"I can't see anything with the exception that there are several people on that list I loved very much."

"I'm sorry. I know how hard that must be."

"I don't see how. Your father's still alive." Remembering brought a very fresh pain of responsibility for Jeremy's accident. *Accident.* Not murder. She was the one who had taken off instead of snorkeling with him. "I'm sorry, Brian, that was rude."

"It's all right. This information is out of the blue from a complete stranger."

"You aren't the first to come to me with this type of conspiracy story. One of Jeremy's friends spread it across

FriendshipConnect. But just like all the others, you can't offer a reason why anyone would want us dead. Nor do you have proof. So…I'm leaving now and I'd appreciate it if you didn't contact me again."

Lindsey threw her bag over her shoulder and left before the sympathetic cowboy could talk her into staying. Her hand found the pepper spray—just in case. Good-looking or not, he had a look in his eyes that promised he wouldn't let this story go. What he'd gain from it…what any of them gained from it, she had no idea and would never understand.

She used her shoulder to push through the door. The afternoon heat wasn't too bad for mid-October. But she was used to much cooler temperatures. Nothing even close to the record-breaking heat wave they'd experienced through the summer in the Dallas–Fort Worth area.

She searched her bottomless pit of a purse until she felt the familiar shape of thick-rimmed sunglasses and pushed them onto her face to block the UV rays. At the next doorway, she ducked under the awning, close to the window, to get out of sight in case Mr. Sloane followed her again.

Someone wanted to murder her? *Ridiculous. Right?*

It didn't make sense. Jeremy had drowned. There were forty other people snorkeling on that reef from his boat. Another twenty-seven from a second tour. They'd all been interviewed and no one had seen anything unusual. Nothing except people snorkeling.

They assumed Jeremy went too deep. From the scratches around his ankle, it looked as though he'd gotten caught on the coral. Nothing foul or sinister. Just tragic.

If I'd been there…I could have prevented his death.

The stinging sensation that preluded tears was just

behind her eyelids. They were seconds away from shedding, just like most days. She watched a couple walk by, shopping bags looped over their shoulders, hands clasped together, no determination in their stride. Perhaps a fun day off?

Maybe she needed a manicure or a sweater since it was beginning to cool down in the evenings?

No. That was the old Lindsey. The one who would take off, not caring if her supervisor got upset, not caring about the job. There was always another job. Not this time. Now she worked regular hours, at a regular job, with the possibility of advancement. There would always be a demand for cell phones, and she was due to start her shift in an hour.

What was here that didn't require spending money? Nothing. It was an outdoor strip mall next to the only real shopping for miles. In fact, her store was just around the corner. She'd have to avoid that section or just be early. She could do that—be early for once. Turn over a new leaf. Take that new start Jeremy wanted for her.

"Okay, then." She left her car parked by Craig's sandwich shop and walked to her boring job.

Seven boring hours later, she rounded the building to empty storefront parking. The lone exception—her car. Jeremy's car, really. The other employees had parked closer and all these shops had closed about an hour before. It was a busy street corner. Lots of traffic, well lit, and she still got a creepy feeling crawling up her spine. She couldn't see anyone. No tall paramedic-psycho-cowboy nearby. She jumped out of her skin when her cell buzzed in her pocket.

Beth.

"Just wanted to make sure you were all right, Lindsey. It seemed like you had a rough day. We all miss him, you know."

"I know. I'm sorry I'm on the verge of crying all the time. There's no mystery why. I live in his apartment. I drive his car. I'm working in the store he managed. I don't just have survivor's guilt because I didn't drown, I'm living his life." She stopped and dug the keys from her purse. "Oh, gosh, I'm sorry to dump on you like that."

"I wouldn't have asked if it wasn't okay. You at your car now?"

Keys in hand, she was close enough to click a button to unlock, she answered, "Yes, I'll see you in a couple of days."

She'd become very used to the little luxuries that had filled her cousin's life. Having a dependable car with hands-free capability was a must from this point forward.

Relaxation would be hers soon. In twenty minutes, she'd be soaking in a hot bath, bubbles up to her chin and lots of candles on the windowsill. There was little traffic on her route home, but a flashing light and detour sign had her turning on an unfamiliar street. Then again. Where was the button for GPS?

The route between apartment and store was easy, but if she got turned around, she could easily get lost on the south side of Arlington. She hadn't been in the area very long and she'd never had a good sense of direction. Another mile and she was so turned around it was silly to try to get back without directions.

No signs at the intersection. She stopped on the right shoulder far enough from the corner to let traffic pass by, then put the car in Park and tapped the screen. The GPS switched on and she looked up in time to see a car approaching behind her. The road was narrow, but with no other cars around, she powered the window down and waved the car to pass her.

The car didn't slow. Was it swerving? Still on a collision course with her. She jammed her foot on the gas. The lights blinded her in the mirror as she sped through the red light.

The impact at the rear of the car was an ear-piercing sound. The jolting crash hurt almost as much as the abrupt stop at the fence post across the street. She closed her eyes and choked when the air bag exploded in her face, feeling the burns shoot across her skin like skidding hard on cement.

By the time she could look up, the only lights around her were from the dashboard. She heard the engine rattling and cut off the ignition. Then nothing. She half expected an evil car to be sitting on the road, racing its engine. But nothing.

All alone.

Sore with every move, she searched for her purse and cell phone, then dialed 911 and explained what had happened.

"Rescue assistance is on the way. Do you want me to stay on the line with you?"

"I'm shook up but I think I'm okay." She reached to disconnect with shaking hands, and that creepy sensation returned. It had sure seemed as if that driver had meant to hit her car. "On second thought, do you mind talking? There aren't any cars around and I…"

"I'd be glad to stay on the line until the police arrive. The squad car is only a couple of minutes out."

Her narrow escape had been close.

Too close?

"Did you see the vehicle that hit you?"

"Not really. No." But it had deliberately swerved onto

the shoulder. She was sure of that. "I think there was a black car following me earlier."

What were the odds of a hit-and-run accident on the very day someone claimed she would be a murder victim?

Should she tell the police about her meeting? What if he actually was the crazy psycho who'd followed? Would they laugh at her like they had Brian? Or was it time to find her own answers? Would anyone believe her except Brian?

"Ma'am? Do you see the police?"

"Yes. Thank you."

She should take charge of her destiny. Take charge. That sounded a lot better than becoming another "accident."

Chapter Three

"Who wants him?" Brian gave the vitals as they came through the emergency room doors. They pushed the gurney to a room where the victim was quickly assessed as stable and blood drawn for an alcohol level. He was the only victim after running a stop sign and causing a multicar pileup in downtown Fort Worth.

"Don't go anywhere, Sloane," his favorite nurse, Meeks, instructed. "After you hand him off, wait for a doctor to stitch up that forehead."

"You know that's not going to happen." He touched the cut and looked at a bloody finger. "Thirty years without stitches and I'm not starting now."

Cam, his rig partner, had laughed when their patient had lashed out, taken him by surprise and knocked him to the floor. Distracted by a pair of sky-blue eyes and convincing himself there was no way to see them again, the drunk John Doe's flaying had sent Brian's forehead into the defibrillator. He hadn't shared the real reason he'd been caught off guard—just complained about the bumps in the road.

He swiped at a drop of blood, keeping it from falling into his eyes.

Meeks ripped open a package and handed him a sterile dressing. "Sit."

"I'm fine."

"You have to wait for the doctor anyway." Meeks pointed to the chair in the corner and Brian sat, applying the dressing to his gash. "You're staying. Wow, he reeks of liquor. It's one of those nights. Someone said it was quiet around here and now we don't have enough doctors."

"Meeks! He's coding," a voice shouted from across the hall.

He could use the E.R. staff owing him a favor. So he waited with his patient while they were called away. Drunk Driver Doe was still out cold and snoring.

"I'm going to clean some of your blood out of the rig. Back in a few."

"I really don't need stitches." He jumped up and spoke to an empty room. At least empty of anyone who could get him out of here.

The gauze quickly soaked with blood. He hadn't taken a good look at it and there weren't any mirrors in the room. So he mentally agreed to wait with Drunk Doe. He looked at the man's vitals again and leaned on the counter. The chair looked more inviting with every throb in his skull. So he sat again.

Closing his eyes, he was immediately immersed in memories of the night of the fire. He hadn't thought about it for twelve years and now that was all he could see. Or hear. Or smell. He and his brother, John, had gone over their movements of the night that had changed their lives so often in the past four months that it played in his head like a movie.

"Sorry I took so long, took me a while to get some coffee. Hey, partner, you okay?" Cam asked, his arms full of their gear. "You're um…dripping."

"You've got to be kidding." Brian was on his feet. The

bloody gauze was on the floor next to him instead of in his hand. "I must have slept a couple of minutes in spite of all the noise around here."

"Passed out's more likely," Meeks added behind Cam.

"Yeah, man. I was gone close to twenty-five minutes. Dispatch is calling, I have to take this." Cam left, answering his cell, his voice fading so fast Brian couldn't hear what he was asked or reporting.

"Sit back down." Meeks donned gloves and assessed his wound, took his BP and asked him standard memory-loss questions. "I'm finding a doctor for those sutures. You're most likely concussed and need a scan."

There was nothing wrong with him except a growing headache—more from all the fuss than injury. But he took it all in stride. If it had been Cam sitting here, he'd have done the same thing. His best efforts to think of another subject led him straight back to his gorgeous bundle of trouble and how to convince her that her life was in danger.

After their first meet, Lindsey Cook thought he was a stalker. He needed to move forward and put the past behind him. Without her. Hadn't he done everything he could do?

So why did he have a bad feeling in the pit of his gut? Why was he trying so hard to convince himself he'd done everything possible? Memories of the town uproar after he'd claimed the fire had been his fault came pressing back to weigh him down. He'd thought he'd done all he could do then, too.

Claiming responsibility for an accident so his brother could continue in the Navy had been the optimal option at the time. But if they'd just talked about that night instead of being so hardheaded, they wouldn't have lost twelve years. Hard years neither of them would get back. Years that had set a chain of events into motion. Not only for him and his twin, but for his family, the ranch, the town and all of Lindsey's family.

If they'd stopped this maniac by forcing the police to discover the truth twelve years ago, how many deaths could have been avoided?

Now he was grateful he'd waited on a doctor. He never wanted to fight with Nurse Meeks. An ironic name for Cindy's demanding personality. Old enough to be his mom, ornery enough to be a prison guard and still loved by everyone who came through her E.R.

A new intern entered pushing a tray. "Are you Sloane?"

"About time. The patient's been unconscious since transport—"

"Wait. I'm not here for him. Meeks said you needed some, um, sutures."

I trust a shaky EMT rookie more than a green first-year med student. "Does Meeks hate me?" If this kid did a terrible job of it, he'd walk out. "Why'd they send you?"

"Everyone else is tied up and they said it would be good practice." He filled a syringe and got the needle ready to deaden Brian's skin.

"Dispatch is ordering you home, buddy," Cam said.

"Ow. Take it easy."

Cam laughed. "Call when you're ready to leave and I'll see if we can swing by and take you back to your truck."

"Come on, Cam. Get one of the real doctors." He kept still while his partner shook his head and covered his laughing hyena mouth. "On second thought, get out. I'll get my own ride back and convince the old man to let me finish my tour."

"Paid leave, man. Take it." Cam patted him on the shoulder and started to leave. "You need to be cleared by a…" He looked the intern over and snickered again. "A real doctor before showing up tomorrow."

Brian was stuck in more ways than one. The strong odor of booze mixed with antiseptic as the intern irrigated the wound, and kind of made him woozy. The kid spun on the little stool and picked up the needle and suture. Then he spun back with shaking hands, seemingly eager to jab the thing into Brian's forehead.

"Hoover Dam, kid!" Brian swatted the intern's fingers away from his head. "Wait for me to deaden up or hand that needle over to me."

"Sorry. We're sort of busy, so I was in a hurry. I forgot."

"Well, go check on a patient or something and come back in a few."

As soon as the kid left, Brian grabbed the needle and planted himself in front of the counter. *Cell phone, flip the camera, instant mirror.* He took a look at the deep gash, couldn't feel anything above his brow and put a couple of clean stitches in the middle.

"Not half-bad," he said to Drunk Doe. He added some tape and was washing his hands when the door opened. "You can tend to your other patients, Doc. I took care of it. You ready to take this patient off my hands?"

He spun around, expecting the intern, but found those sad blue eyes that had haunted him for weeks.

"Hi. I bet this seems strange to track you down in the middle of the night," Lindsey Cook said, as if she hadn't threatened a restraining order that afternoon.

"A little. I didn't think I'd see you again after this afternoon." The abrasions on her face screamed for him to ask, but she'd sought him out for some reason. Maybe he should wait to ask, but her face was ashen. If he wasn't mistaken, she was in a great deal of pain.

"They said you'd been injured and might need a ride home." She sounded less confident. Almost afraid.

"Don't take this the wrong way, but you don't look so hot yourself."

"I'm fine." She sat on the rolling stool he'd just vacated. "So you really are an EMT."

He didn't want to correct her on the difference between an EMT and paramedic. "Yeah, I am. How'd you find me?" *More important, why did you want to?*

"I called a Fort Worth fire station and asked for you. One fireman was kind enough to explain that the ambulance service is a different company. I found the number and they assumed I was your sister-in-law for some odd reason. I didn't bother to correct them."

The shy smile she shot his direction didn't hide that she'd lied to find him. She reached to push her hair behind her ear and winced. Even an untrained person could figure out she was hurt.

"I guess it didn't dawn on my colleagues that my sister-in-law would just call my cell." He tapped his phone still on the counter.

"Not if she had a surprise. But they assumed you were getting a CT scan or something and couldn't answer your phone."

He pointed to his head. "No scan for me. So why didn't you just call me? You had the number."

"Well, I wanted to have this conversation face-to-face."

So she'd done her own amateur detective work, found him and had something to say. The room was a little small, throwing them within touching distance. Something he'd wanted more of since shaking her hand that afternoon.

"I'm sorry for frightening you today. I just thought

you'd want to know," he said to start the conversation again. The intern would be returning soon and it would be even more awkward.

She seized his hand, clinging to it with a sense of desperation he knew all too well. The desperate need for someone to care and make you feel like you weren't alone. He'd been there four months ago when his father had suffered a major stroke.

"I think someone tried to kill me tonight," she whispered, her eyes darting to the drunk on the bed.

"What happened?" He moved to lean on the counter. Nothing jerky, but it shifted her arm.

She released a sharp hiss between her teeth. "I got lost on the way to Jeremy's house and—"

"Hey, first things first. Did you see a doctor? Where are you injured?"

"My shoulder's hurting. It's just bruised from the seat belt."

"Mind if I have a look?" His fingers were already heading toward her.

"Do you really know what you're doing?"

He had to laugh. "Yeah, I've been doing this over eight years now. More if you count all the horses on the ranch I've nursed back to health." When she turned those baby blues on him he had trouble focusing. "You didn't answer me. Did anyone look at your shoulder, and how long ago did it happen?"

"The EMT checked it around ten. And another doctor at the E.R. I'll be fine."

Seat belt injury equaled car wreck. He gently probed her left shoulder through her shirt where the strap would have bruised. "So you got lost and had an accident?"

"I don't think it was an accident," she whispered again.

She didn't jerk away, just looked at Drunk Doe. "Is it safe to talk here?"

"He's unconscious. We have plenty of time to go over what happened while I get one of the doctors to examine you."

"No. Please. I've already been to the emergency room. It's okay, really." She caught his hand again. "Does that mean you'll help me? You're the only one who might believe me."

"What can I do? I'm a paramedic, not a bodyguard."

Brian wanted the truth, but attempted murder was out of his league. He had other problems to think about anyway. His twin brother was home for good and married with a kid. His family's ranch was getting closer to foreclosure. And he wanted to say yes so badly to this woman his mouth was forming the word.

"If someone tried to kill you, then the police are working your case. I should probably stay out of it."

The relief rushed his body like a warm shower. He could focus on finding the money to take over the ranch payments. Maybe stop working as a paramedic and focus on breeding champion quarter horses again. Maybe see a little more of the world. Maybe watch some Sunday football. Buy a boat and get some fishing in. Lots of boring choices instead of working every minute.

Nothing like his brother's life as a Navy SEAL. And none of which involved spending time with a beautiful blonde.

"I hate saying this, Brian, but I'm afraid to go home alone. I need your help. You're my only hope."

"I'm not a hero in some movie. I'm a nobody." He pushed on her shoulder to make sure it was in place. "I think it's just bruised. Did they get an X-ray? I'll call a nurse."

"Wait." She latched on to his biceps. "You're the only reason my car didn't shoot into a telephone poll. Your warning made me extracautious and I kept watching the car behind me. If you hadn't spoken to me this afternoon, I wouldn't need your help now. I'd be dead."

He was dang tired of being anyone's *only hope.* His brother twelve years ago. The ranch. His dad. He'd warned her. That was all he could do. "This is a job for the police, not an amateur with some friends who did some digging for him."

"But they won't. The police officer called it an accident and blamed me for not pulling farther off the road." Those picture-perfect eyes filled to their full mark and one tear escaped down her tanned, freckled cheek. She swiped at it with the back of her free hand.

"God-d…bless America." He couldn't say yes. "This is such a bad idea. I'm not the guy you need to help you."

"But you're the one who told me—"

"I'm going to have a doctor look at your shoulder." Brian gently cupped her injury, gave it a soft you'll-be-all-right pat and grabbed the door with every intention to march into the hall, shout for Meeks and continue his life. But that nagging gut feeling wouldn't let him. "What is it you want me to do?"

"Tell me how to convince the authorities someone's after me."

"I haven't had much luck with that."

Was this the same woman he'd met earlier, so full of confidence protecting herself at the sandwich shop? Injured, sitting with her shoulders slumped, waiting on answers he didn't have. If he hadn't put the idea of murder into her life, she wouldn't be afraid to go home. It would have been just another car accident.

Another accident.

"How do you know it was deliberate? You're certain the car swerved off the road? Were there any witnesses?"

"I can tell when a car swerves directly toward me." She sat straight with confidence. "How did you get that cut on your forehead?"

Leave. Forget Miss Blue Eyes and your curiosity. You can't do anything to help.

"I fell." His hand was still on the door handle. "Why?"

"Any witnesses?" She rubbed her shoulder. "I'm sure the police will believe you. It shouldn't be a problem, but you could have been in a fight. Or drunk. Lord knows you smell like you bathed in alcohol."

"Got me. You didn't mention to the cop at the scene about your family history? Or that I think the family accidents might actually be murders?"

She pressed her lips together, shook her head and nervously raised a finger to twist her hair. "I sort of told them, but they wouldn't believe me when I said I didn't know who you were."

"You had my number and I could have confirmed your details. Why wouldn't you? Oh, I get it. You think if you tell the cops that I'll be in trouble?"

"Hey," she said, standing and putting a hand on a hip. "I don't know what to believe. Right now, I'm exhausted but there's no way I can go home alone. No, no, no, you get that look out of your eyes, mister. I'm not asking you to come home with me. Shoot. I sort of thought you might have been the guy who hit me. I don't think you are, since the other firemen confirmed your shift began at seven. But honestly, I don't know you."

"Did you hit your head?"

"No. At least, I don't think I did. The air bag scraped me."

He watched the realization of his words wash over her in an embarrassing shade of pink.

"Oh, no. I'm sorry. When I get nervous, I tend to babble. I think you misunderstood what I meant earlier."

"What part? When you asked for help? Or when you thought I might have tried to murder you?"

"All I want is a cup of coffee and some pancakes." She cradled her arm closer to her side.

Pancakes? He could go for some pancakes. "Cafeteria's closed. Will Pan-Hop do?" Maybe she could fill in some blanks in his research?

She nodded. "Great. I love their double-stack special. What about him?"

"I almost forgot about Drunk Driver Doe." He pressed the nurse call button. "Meeks. I've gotta leave."

"I'll be right there, Sloane."

"For the record," Lindsey said with the confidence he'd seen when they'd first met, "I don't know why I started looking for you, but this seemed like my only option. I don't intend to have any more *accidents*."

"The folder's in my truck back at the lot. My captain's already told me to head home." He pointed to his bandage. "Get me pancakes and I'll tell you everything."

"My moment of feeling sorry for myself is over. I want all the details. Everything you've learned about my family."

He could pass along what he'd discovered. Maybe not everything. He couldn't admit that he'd been admiring her gorgeous body since seeing her picture on her website four months ago. Probably better to keep that information to himself. At least for a while.

And why today? If this guy waits years, planning his murders to disguise them as accidents, then why attempt a hit and run? Had he brought Lindsey to the murderer's attention? Or worse, sped up his timetable?

How could he walk away if he was responsible?

Chapter Four

Lindsey restrained herself through the short drive, asking only how Brian had received the cut. He'd laughed as he'd said to avoid an inexperienced intern with over-eager fingers, he'd stitched it himself. But the story had left her queasy after dropping him off at the ambulance company's home base. The Pan-Hop was right around the corner.

While she waited, the memory of the car lights blinded her again. The awful thought that her life had been about to end replayed over and over. Because of Brian's visit earlier that day, she was still alive. She'd only been alone waiting for him to arrive about five minutes before a tap on the window made her jump out of her skin.

"You ready to go inside?" Brian asked.

She grabbed her purse and locked the car. He'd changed into the street clothes he'd worn when they'd met that afternoon. A lifetime ago. She hadn't noticed his scuffed boots until he'd held the door and she'd looked to the ground. The only boots she'd noticed before were on men shopping for a new phone. She hadn't been in Texas too long and hadn't made an effort to get to know anyone or discover any real cowboys.

Now one had found her.

He waited, holding the restaurant door open while

she looked past him through the windows. Any of those people could have been driving the car that rammed her off the road. It could be anyone…anywhere.

A creepy feeling crawled up her spine. He was out there. She could feel him staring from his hiding place. Pure panic drove her. She spun and searched the dark.

"We going to eat?"

"I can't." Darting under his arm, she began clicking the rental's key, trying to unlock the door. The car alarm set the horn blaring and she looked closer to see which button was which, but her eyes were full of embarrassing tears.

Tears? Now? She'd remained calm throughout the accident and police. But couldn't handle pancakes in a public place.

Brian clasped his hands over hers, tilted her chin toward him and took the keys. The alarm stopped, then she heard the horn beep that it was reset. He hadn't looked away. His dark eyes reassured something deep inside. More than basic attraction, sort of as though he shared part of her no one else could—or would—ever understand.

Even with his eyes comforting her, the panic bubbled. She looked into the dark corners of the building, right at the edge of the light. He was there, watching.

"What's wrong?"

"I can't go in there, it's…it's too crowded." Her mind acknowledged that the restaurant was more than half-empty, but it just didn't matter. She couldn't force her feet to move through the entrance.

Brian seemed to understand. He led her by the elbow to his truck, opened the door and removed a bag from the floor. "Want me to help you inside?"

It was an older model and it took a little doing one-handed, but she managed to climb in on her own.

"Mind if I hook you up? This thing can be sort of stubborn." He pulled and held the seat belt forward.

She nodded and he leaned across the seat. She would never have been able to lift her arm to lock herself in and he'd helped without her asking. He smelled of a mixture of hay and man. Attractive. Musky. Like a guy who did honest work or who'd driven with the top down on a bright sunny day.

His hair was short, but didn't look like his normal style since he kept tossing his head as though there were longer locks there. She recognized that toss of his head and the nervous running of his fingers across his scalp. She did it herself to get short wisps away from her face. It looked as if it was growing out from a military cut close to his head, curling at the base of his neck.

He hadn't been exaggerating when he'd said the seat belt was stubborn. It wasn't just a play to get closer. His hands touched her hip more than once and as hard as he tried not to, his arm grazed her stomach and thigh.

The urge to twist those curls around her finger was a little heady. She'd acted on impulse before. It would be so easy to reach out and use her nail to trace the lean tendon leading down to his shoulder.

She watched her hand sort of float down, getting closer to that musky skin.

"There." He stood straight, brushing her hand to the side with his shoulder, smiling from ear to ear as though he'd accomplished something much harder than snapping a seat belt. "Dang thing had an animal cracker stuck in it."

"Great." She didn't feel great. Maybe she had hit her head because she was definitely a little dizzy. He seemed perfectly fine and totally unaffected by all the touching.

"Your shoulder okay?" he asked, adjusting the strap to make it a little looser while holding an animal cracker tight in his palm. He was thinking of his niece, not her. He just wanted her to be safe while in his truck.

Shoot, he was a paramedic. He probably got hit on all the time. Girls probably fell at his feet. Well, that was the old Lindsey. The new Lindsey didn't fall at anyone's feet. She used her own. The tenseness she felt had nothing to do with the physical and everything to do with the potential threat on her life.

Anyone would feel like this.

"Great, thanks. Your mother must be very proud of raising such a gentleman."

The smile faded from his eyes and his lips twisted tightly into a thin line. He quickly shut the door. "Mom died of cancer a long time ago," he said softly through the open window.

He walked around the back of the truck, pausing to drop the bag in the back and again at the door. His face was out of sight, but she heard the deep inhale and slow release.

Trying to pay him a compliment, she'd brought up a terrible pain. She knew all about the death of a parent and felt two inches tall for the remark she'd made about him still having his father when they'd first met.

He got in and pulled from the parking lot. "Don't feel bad, Lindsey. You didn't know."

"I meant it as a compliment."

"And that's how I took it. She's been gone a long time."

"My parents' accident was six years ago. When I remember that day…all the horrible feelings make me hurt all over. I can't imagine it ever gets easier."

"It does and it doesn't. Hang on to the good stuff." He shifted gears and stopped at a red light.

The streets were practically empty. She looked around for a black car, trying not to but paranoid. Each time they stopped, she searched.

"I doubt he's going to do anything when you're with me. This guy makes it look like an accident. That's why no one's caught on. So where do you live?"

"You must already know, since you're headed there. It's really okay. I looked up a couple of things about you, too. The fire did more than kill my cousin. It destroyed all your plans and your family's. I think it's cool that you're an identical twin. You might have told me what happened this summer. Your story made the news. And your poor little niece."

"You didn't seem too receptive to more talking this afternoon. Were the articles and pictures helpful?"

"Yes. You can't blame me for checking out your story. You could have been driving the car that ran me off the road for all I knew."

"And yet, you didn't tell the cops my name."

"How did you know?"

"I don't seem to be in police custody on suspicion of murder."

"Right. The police already thought I was drunk or high or just crazy. Then there was the mess when they thought I'd stolen Jeremy's car. *That* took forever to clear up. So I let them take me home and used the internet."

"Wait, go back. They thought you stole a car?"

"That's beside the point, but if you must know, Jeremy left me his car. I've been making the payments. The bank wouldn't put it in my name. When I told the cop at the accident that the owner was dead…" She rubbed the scratches she'd gotten from the handcuffs they used while escorting her to the police station to sort things out. "Part of the reason it was so late when I found you was that it took a long time to find Jeremy's lawyer and verify everything."

"Is this your place?"

"Jeremy's, really."

"If it's got a lock on the door, you'll be fine. Want me to walk you to the door?"

"Yes. I mean, aren't we going to talk? You can tell me what your plans are. How do you plan to catch this guy? Oh, wait, we should talk inside. But what if it's bugged or something?"

"Lindsey." He lifted a hand as a universal stop sign. "Lindsey, slow down. I'm not that guy."

He reached forward and gently popped her seat belt loose. At some point he'd already undone his and twisted on the old vinyl. Draping his arm over the back of the seat, he rested his head in his hand.

He arched his brows, waiting, but she didn't know how to respond. She didn't completely understand the question, so what did he want?

"Look, kid—"

"Stop right there. I'm not a kid. You can't be more than three or four years older than me. Remember, I did research on you, too. So I'm not your kid, sweetheart, baby, doll or whatever nickname you can create. My name's Lindsey."

"Yes ma'am. Like I was saying, I'm not the guy you want defending you. I have no resources, no knowledge, no experience or desire to protect you. You need someone who knows what they're doing."

"But who else is going to believe me, Brian?"

"You've got me there. I had a helluva time just getting myself to believe me. Then Mabel did some research and all those accidents didn't seem so accidental."

"You'll help?" She focused on his eyes, the slight tilt

of his mouth that was much more comforting than those tight, strained lips.

"I don't know what I can do, *Lindsey,* but I'll tell you what I know. Stay there and I'll help you out before you hurt that shoulder again. The muscles are probably stiffening up about now."

He scooped the folder from the seat and she waited while he walked around the truck. If he wanted to be gallant, she'd let him. Allowing him to open the door for her wasn't being a pushover—especially if he wasn't doing any pushing.

She creaked to the edge and stepped down. Brian was right. She ached all over.

"Aw, I told you."

The wince had probably given her away. She would have stumbled to the ground if he hadn't been there helping. "I can't believe how sore I am all of a sudden."

"The adrenaline's wearing off and I bet you'll be out as soon as your head hits the pillow."

"No way. We have things to discuss. I want to know everything you know."

"And I'll be here in the morning. Does that perplexed look indicate you don't know if it's a good idea or not?"

"I just… I mean, just because I tracked you down doesn't mean I invited you to spend the night." *Remember, someone's trying to kill you.* A little voice in her head, sounding so much like Jeremy, kept reminding her to look around. The paranoia had her doubting Brian's motives.

"I thought we were past all that. I didn't try to kill you. You can trust me."

Fear made her anxious. She could feel it trying to take over again. Then Jeremy's voice prodded her, *You need his help. What about your mother and father's accident?*

*You may have been murdered. You need to find the truth
and this guy's already found a great deal. Don't stop until
you get the psycho who's been destroying our family.*

She scraped her scalp with the metal key ring still in
her palm as she shoved her hand through her hair. She'd
been doing so well on her own. She shook her head,
wanting the answer to be different than what was obvious. She couldn't do this on her own. Good or bad, she
needed him.

"I'm sorry. This situation is just a little overwhelming." She stretched her neck back to get a look at the most
comforting eyes she'd ever fallen into. They made her
next words much easier to say, "Would you mind staying awhile? I'd feel safer."

He held out his hand for her keys. She'd promised herself never to ask for help again. Did this count?

THE KEYS DROPPED into Brian's palm and they moved inside with no more debate. Lindsey was obviously on her
last ounce of energy, stumbling out of her shoes and falling onto the leather couch.

"Why don't you head to bed?" He flipped on lights,
set the file on the coffee table and wanted to remove his
boots. If he could just close his eyes for a few... The exhaustion from his shift was intensifying the pounding
behind his eyes from the slight concussion.

"I'm so wound up, I really don't think I can go to
sle..." She stopped, staring at the goldfish tank on the
corner of the desk.

"What's the matter?"

She moved next to him, no longer wilting. "Someone's been here," she whispered. "Could they still be in
the house?"

"How can you tell?" He pulled her close under his arm, as if that would actually protect her if someone attacked.

"The fish-food container was on top of Jeremy's papers. Not next to the bowl. Feeding them was one of the last things I did before I left this morning." Her whispering voice shook with fright as much as her body shook under his hand.

"You're certain?"

"Yes."

"We're leaving."

"But—"

"Now, Lindsey. Out."

She turned and ran. He didn't linger. He wanted to check things out. Might have if he'd been alone. But he wasn't. For whatever it was worth, Lindsey had chosen him as her protector and he'd do his best. That did not include a fool idea that he should seek out trouble.

Trouble had a way of finding him all on its own.

When he pulled away from her home, Lindsey explored her purse until she removed her cell. "Shoot, my battery's nearly dead. Can I use your phone?"

"I don't think calling anyone is a good idea. Let's talk first and come up with a game plan. Sound good?"

"But what about prints or stuff like that?"

"I don't think this guy left any sign he's been in your house. He's been pretty darn good about covering his tracks."

"Okay, we'll play it your way right now. Just know that this is my life and if *I* decide to make a call, I will." She hugged her sore shoulder close to her chest.

"Absolutely." He pulled to a stop and snapped her belt. "It's over an hour to my place. You can use my jacket for a pillow. One of us should get some sleep."

He drove the truck, trying not to be distracted as she

shifted and got comfortable without another word. Hell, he'd shut down for months when he'd thought John had accidentally started a fire that had killed Mrs. Cook. He couldn't really fathom what it would be like to have someone try to kill him.

"Thank you, Brian."

"You're welcome. Now try to get some shut-eye."

He should force her to go back to the police or hire someone who could help. Taking her to the ranch seemed the easiest choice he'd made recently. Since he and John had cleared the air and actually talked about the night that had changed their lives forever, decisions he'd made on his own for years about the ranch were suddenly up for a group discussion.

For four months he'd craved catching the murdering son of a bitch who had destroyed his future. Now it was more important than ever. He couldn't leave Lindsey to handle this on her own.

The hour zoomed by—even in the old Ford his grandfather had bought and used for fifteen years. Brian tinkered with the engine, keeping it running smoothly. It might not have AC, but it was his. The bank couldn't repossess it like they were trying to foreclose on the ranch.

One trouble at a time.

Keeping Lindsey alive was more important than finding a way to buy the ranch. He turned down the drive, cut the lights and parked next to the barn. Lindsey was still out. She mumbled a little when he shifted her to open the door.

The wind had blown her hair across her face. He leaned close, gently blowing the small strands to the side. He couldn't resist. His lips grazed her forehead so softly he wasn't certain he'd connected with her flesh until his lips cooled again. He scooped her up in his arms, cradling her head in the crook of his shoulder.

He was behaving like a sentimental and romantic idiot. He knew all there was about Lindsey Cook. More than he wanted or needed to know. No way would she go for a cowboy like him. He wasn't anywhere near her league of resort-hopping rich and didn't know how to get there. Didn't want to get there.

Dawn was just around the corner. Time for the morning chores, and no extra hands to do any part of them. What would this beach bunny think of his family's ranch?

The old house needed a coat of paint. The barn needed a new roof. The stock tank needed to be dredged. And there were hardly enough horses left to be considered a farm anymore. It wasn't anything to show off, but it was his.

Or could be. He'd done a lot of thinking since John had come home. Since he turned fifteen, the one thing he'd been talking about doing was leaving this small piece of real estate. Now he couldn't figure out a way to keep from being kicked off the place.

Brian got through the door without the screen slamming shut, a sleeping beauty still in his arms.

"I thought your shifts were for three days?" His brother yawned and scratched his head coming into the kitchen. "Want coffee?"

John finally looked up from the pot that had automatically kicked on and brewed. He pointed and raised an eyebrow, recognition at Lindsey's identity twisting his face into shock, then anger.

Brian was tired and didn't want to wake his new responsibility with loud voices or explanations.

"Don't ask, bro. Just don't ask."

Chapter Five

Serendipity at its best. He could do nothing except admire how the universe worked to bring him back to the only man to have received acclaim for one of his masterpieces.

The Sloane brothers had been the perfect pawns. He'd switched on the voice-activated microphone he'd installed years ago to record his work. There would come a day when someone would transcribe his dictation and print his book, *Details of a Successful Serial Killer*.

"Will Brian Sloane's primitive investigation cause problems for your last plan?" He asked himself the question as if a reporter sat in the room. "The paramedic is a growing pain in the ass and will be eliminated as soon as the opportunity arises."

After he was gone, someone should know what he'd accomplished. There shouldn't be any supposition regarding each case. When the world discovered his lifelong achievements, it should be in his own words.

The idea came to him after the second successful death. Each plan was chronicled and stored in a fireproof safe once completed, but there was nothing like hearing about the conceptualization or nuances that made each one different to execute.

"But that wasn't the question, sir." The reporter in his mind continued to dig. "Will he present a problem?"

For several years, he'd been using the recording device like an audible journal. At first, it had been to document his work. Basically, he was so good at creating *accidents* that no one knew he'd done anything.

"Keeping track of the Sloane brothers for twelve years hasn't been difficult. They lead uneventful lives with the exception of John's return home. He set off a chain of very unfortunate events. That has only forced me to accelerate my plans for the last Cook family member. With Lindsey's death, there are no claims on what's been mine for many years now."

He pushed away from his desk, preferring the supple leather of his couch for what amounted to a debate with himself to logically reason his way through a new challenge.

"If those laughable amateurs who kidnapped Lauren Adams hadn't gotten greedy, the Sloanes would never have discovered my craftsmanship with the Cook deaths. Hiding Gillian's murder within the barn fire was convenient, but also brilliant. I was so close to perfection."

He opened and poured a shot of his favorite vodka. He needlessly swirled it in the cut glass, waiting for the right moment to consume.

"To recap, Gillian checked on the fire pit each time those high school children left her property. One swing of a board and she was unconscious as the barn burned around her. Convenient, yet brilliant. No one has ever discovered the truth of her murder."

There was a right moment for everything. People had forgotten the art of patience. Waiting made the win worth savoring.

"I'll need to get rid of them both. Soon, and without a lot of fuss." He downed the clear shot. One was his limit.

He enjoyed the burning sensation as it traveled through his body, immediately craving more of the fiery liquid.

"No, there isn't a problem. But I am conflicted. Arranging a major accident would get the entire ranch out of my way for good, yet forcing an accident on their ranch is irrational. There would be too many witnesses. The pertinent question is, how do I get Brian and Lindsey to leave the ranch?"

He brushed the back of his finger under his mustache, verifying no drops of liquid moistened his upper lip. Reaching for the bottle, he realized the cool glass was in his hand and shouldn't be. He slammed it on the table, shooting drops in the air that landed on the polished wood.

"How can I overcome this setback? Strike that. I consider this puzzle a welcome challenge. I haven't had any in many years." He leaned into the leather, resting his head, focusing on the microphone in the ceiling tiles. Closing his eyes, he pictured the horse ranch where Sloane had taken Lindsey. It was the only logical place he could go. He envisioned the buildings and the distances, places to hide, the horses and where they wandered.

"I have to admit, this challenge is the first time I've desired to meet my opponent face-to-face. If the opportunity presents itself, I might consider doing so. But that's part of the beauty of this operation. No one knows. Not even my victims knew I controlled whether they lived or died."

He'd given his word to himself and anyone listening to these tapes that they'd always be completely truthful. The last murder had been slightly different than the rest.

"Addendum. Pathetic Jeremy Cook most likely saw a distorted image through his snorkeling face mask. That was the closest I've ever gotten to any of my victims.

When I was within striking distance, he was still completely at ease. My sheer strength kept him underwater. Fear never showed in his eyes until the last bubble of air escaped from his lungs. Then he knew. He knew there was no escape."

Reliving the experience made his heart race and made him need more of the same exhilarating excitement. He wouldn't put that on the tapes. Doctors or the media would twist the pleasure he took from a well-executed plan. They'd distort it and turn his excellence into something sick that needed analysis.

"Back to the problem at hand. How to eliminate the Cook line and take care of the Sloanes with the same deed." The map of the property was firmly in his mind even after twelve years. As were the images of each building, the road, the fields, the pond…all there, creating a secret thrill he couldn't share. He ran the idea from start to finish.

Excitement. Anticipation. Reward.

"Brilliant. Yes, a tip to the press connecting Brian to a possible hit-and-run accident will work nicely. A photographer should spook them sufficiently to where they are alone and vulnerable. I'll record the details upon completion. There's no need to repeat myself in dictation."

Some men were thrilled by the hunt. Some by the kill. He poured another shot. It was time to celebrate. He held the glass in the air.

"A toast. To twenty years of excellence in murder."

The vodka did its job, and he rose to switch off the recorder. There was one part of himself that he refused to share with the world. They'd label him perverted if they discovered his need to hear the moans of torture. He hid his tendency, only allowing himself to indulge as a reward for his greatness.

Fate had stepped in and brought him an opponent for his last plan. His own intelligence would be Lindsey's downfall, and deserved to be fed and stroked. Seeing the report of another assumed overdosed prostitute in the news would meet his growing need for acknowledgment. It would also satisfy him in other pleasurable areas while she or he died.

The perfect subject for his reward had already been chosen and would fit into his plans nicely. But not a random death on the street. He had the perfect place to carry out his deed.

The celebration after his Cozumel success had been near Jeremy's home. With Lindsey secure with the Sloanes, it might be risky to return there. But Jeremy's bed would make the satisfaction all the sweeter.

Chapter Six

Brian's head throbbed. He was tired. Not just from hitting his temple earlier. He needed sleep and a couple of days off. It seemed like years since he'd sat down and wasn't on the clock, looking at ranch records or researching murders. Recently, the spare hours he'd had between shifts were spent following Lindsey's every move. His bed looked very inviting. His father's bed even more so with Miss Blue Eyes curled under the sheets now.

If he was lucky, he'd be under some sheets with her fairly soon. She had to be feeling the chemical reaction every time they were in the same room. Right? Hitting the hay with her could happen once they knew each other better, but not here. Not with a houseful of his family around.

The rooster crowed at the first peek of dawn. He might as well help with the morning feeding for once since he was up. It beat balancing the ranch books. Changed and gulping down a cup of coffee, he caught up with John halfway through feeding the stabled horses.

"Ready to tell me what's going on?" his brother asked.

"There was an accident."

"You didn't do anything stupid, did you? We talked about this." John sounded like an older brother or more like a former Naval officer used to getting answers.

"I didn't do a damn thing, John. Lay off." He pushed his hat to the back of his head. "And stop lecturing me every time we have a conversation. I've been taking care of this place for twelve years."

"What the hell happened to your head?" John's hands framed Brian's face, turning it so he could get a closer look. His thumbs stretched the laceration, tugging at the bandage. "You're bleeding."

"Blast it, John. Stop treating me like I'm ten." Brian shook free and swiped at his forehead. "I've got a father and don't need you to baby me."

Sometime during the past four months they'd switched their traditional roles. Identical in every visible way, Brian had always been the responsible one, older by minutes but by light-years in responsibility. The complete opposite of John's jokester personality. His little brother had finally grown up while in the Navy. Or maybe it was coming home, making amends with his high school sweetheart and planning to adopt her daughter.

"Whoever stitched you up did a crappy job, bro. That's going to leave a scar. And don't think *I'm* slicing my forehead so we can switch places again."

"Seems as though every time we've switched it was your idea and I was getting *you* out of trouble."

"Don't change the subject. What happened?" John stepped back, stiffening, as if he was at attention, commanding his men. It was obvious he wasn't continuing with scooping oats until he got an answer. "After you went to the cops and they laughed in your face, I thought we agreed that it was over."

"Stand down. This ain't the Navy, man. Nothing major happened to me. This is from a drunk in my rig." He straightened his hat. "Lindsey's the one who had an accident. She's a little freaked to be alone, that's all. I brought her here. That's it. No big deal. Now, I'm awful tired, so why don't we get through the chores and I'll explain after breakfast. Once. To everyone. Alicia will be home and Dad can pretend that he's been home all night. Right, Dad?"

His father popped his head around the open double doors leading to the paddock. "I didn't want to interrupt."

"You're not interrupting. Maybe Blue Eyes will be awake for your interrogation. That work for everybody?"

"Blue Eyes?" John and his dad questioned together, sounding so much alike it was creepy.

"Yeah, Lindsey."

"You agreed to leave this alone. What happened twelve years ago doesn't matter." John picked up the scoop and measured oats for the horses.

"It matters to me. And I never agreed. You ordered and I reminded you that I don't take orders from you."

Brian left each bucket in a different stall, feeding the trained quarter horses he'd been trying to sell for months. He was ready to move to the next chore when John began laughing. "What's so dang funny?"

"It just occurred to me, you put those stitches in yourself. Right?" He slapped his thighs, stumbling back a couple of steps, laughing hard at his own joke. "I knew it."

"What stitches?" his dad asked, leaning on his cane. Not bad for a man recovering from a major stroke four months ago. He walked a good two miles every day just coming home from Mabel's across the street.

"John's losing his mind. Glad you're here to take care of him if he starts convulsing." Brian lengthened his stride to leave faster. "I'm going to make breakfast."

"We need to talk about the ranch, boy-o," his father said loudly. "The bank called again."

"Can't right now, Dad. I have a date with the griddle."

Brian left as John expounded on the crooked sutures. If his brother noticed, it was probably a good idea to let his sister-in-law, the professional nurse in the family, redo his sutures.

Right now, he was starved and needed to get his mind off some sky-blue eyes and corn-silk hair spread over a pillow in the front bedroom.

"Yum. Pancakes."

The distinct smell of a hot griddle and syrup wafted into Lindsey's nose, encouraging her to breathe deeply and enjoy. She stretched her arms above her head. No surfing today, her shoulder was a little sore. She rubbed it as she sank back into the pillows, surrounded by the comforting feeling of her favorite place in Florida. The sun streamed through the windows every morning and she'd breathe in the soft, fresh smell of sun-dried sheets. There was a plus side to not owning a dryer.

Snuggling the quilt closer to her chest, she wanted to spend the rest of the morning asleep. But there was work or something she was supposed to do. And pancakes. Her eyes fluttered open to an unfamiliar room.

Wide-awake in an instant. Panic. Aches.

Where am I?

Then her memory kicked in with Brian's words that he was taking her to his home. Darn. She was on a ranch, not back at the beach. She'd be inside the storefront cage where she worked by three that afternoon. Stuck inside. It couldn't compare to working in the sun, walking in the sand or having the surf as part of every conversation.

She missed the sun. But she was responsible now, with a real job and possible advancement. A permanent roof over her head instead of crashing with relatives during the winter season when she was broke. Responsibility was a good thing.

The room didn't look like Brian at all. Pictures in old frames were placed on a dresser around a handmade doily and jewelry box. Grandparents, baby photos of two identical boys and a stunning woman in a wedding dress from the 70s. Either the loner she'd met wasn't much of a loner or it wasn't Brian's room after all.

She was still completely dressed except for her shoes—a good thing, no awkward moments. She made the bed like a good guest—she'd been one often enough. Hit the bathroom, then not wanting to disturb anyone, she tiptoed through the hallway leading to the living area. She followed the heavenly smell of pancakes, hoping to find her cowboy rescuer.

A man was crashed on the couch. His face was pressed into the back cushions, but she knew it was Brian. His boots were at one end with his hat resting on top. She wasn't surprised he was still asleep. He'd worked all night, then stayed up with her. What she couldn't believe was that he'd carried her to bed and she hadn't woken up.

"Shh. You'll get in trouble if you wake up Uncle Brian," a little girl tried to whisper from the kitchen entrance, placing her first finger across her lips but speaking loud enough to be heard across the room.

Lindsey followed the little girl into the kitchen, hesitating before interrupting the woman cleaning up, uncertain how to explain why she was in her home. These two had to be the new additions to the family. She recognized their pictures from the articles she'd found involving Brian and the little girl's kidnapping last summer.

"Mommy," Brian's niece said, sending her pigtails bouncing over her shoulders.

"Lauren, you know you have to eat before you can

go outside. Get back in your seat and leave Uncle Brian alone." She didn't look away from the dishes in the sink.

"Brian's lady is up," she announced, and her mom turned. Lauren laced her fingers through Lindsey's and tugged her across the kitchen. Mother and daughter looked alike; both had rich, dark brown hair and the same arch to their brows.

"Hi, I'm Alicia. Brian said y'all got here at dawn. I didn't expect you up this soon." Alicia wiped her hands on a dish towel. There had been a moment of hesitation with her smile, but it looked genuine now that it was in place. Then she knelt by her daughter. "Lauren, you didn't go and wake Miss Lindsey up, did you?"

Another surprise, Alicia Sloane knew her name. "Oh, no, I had a great sleep," Lindsey rushed to explain. "I met Lauren in the living room. Oh, and I'm not Brian's lady. We just met yesterday and he brought me here because I had no place to go. Great, that sort of sounds horrible. I mean, the story's a little complicated. A lot complicated, actually."

Alicia smiled bigger, stood and tapped Lauren on the bottom, scooting her toward her booster seat at the table. "Thank you for minding me, sweetie. Now get up there and finish eating. Don't worry, Lindsey. Brian explained everything over breakfast. Are you hungry? I was instructed to give you hotcakes as soon as you were ready."

"They smell delicious. Can I help?"

"Guests don't cook, silly." One of the cutest giggles she'd ever heard came from tiny lips and a mouth full of pancakes.

"Lauren, that was rude. You don't call grown-ups silly." Brian's sister-in-law retrieved the batter from the refrigerator and slid it onto the mixer stand. "And you don't talk with your mouth full."

"But you do. You said Uncle Brian bringing a guest to Pawpaw's very full house was silly." She folded another half of a small pancake and stuffed it in her mouth, smiling with a drip of syrup on her chin as she chewed.

"Oh, gosh." Alicia's hand covered her cheeks. "I'm so sorry."

"It's okay. You're right, me being here is quite silly. Um…" Lindsey understood. Staying here wasn't only awkward for the Sloanes. She had a bit of background, but what did she really know about Brian? "I guess I should go. If you know where my purse is, I'll call a cab to take me home."

"Don't be silly," Alicia said. "Oh, my, there I go again. What I meant to say is you're more than welcome to stay here as long as you want. This is Brian's house more than mine, and I shouldn't have spouted off about a lack of space. Lauren, we'll talk about this later, young lady."

"I really think I should go." She backed up, trying to leave gracefully. Maybe she'd missed her purse in Brian's room. Two strong hands cupped her shoulders, steadying her as she tripped into a rock-solid body.

"You've got nowhere to go. Remember?" Brian's voice said just above her head.

"Are you in trouble, Mommy? Uncle Brian looks mad."

"I'm tired, baby girl. Just tired." His warm breath tickled her spine. "I get ornery when I only get a half hour of shut-eye."

"I told you to sleep in our room," Alicia said.

"That will never happen." He laughed. "Don't worry about it. I function on naps all the time. Besides, the smell of that griddle made me hungry again." He patted Lindsey's shoulders and guided her to a chair at the old-fashioned table. "How's the shoulder?"

"A little sore, but fine."

The strange part of the scene around her was that she didn't feel unwanted or a burden or even more than slightly awkward. When Brian was in the room, she felt at home. Her hand skimmed the table top as he pushed her chair closer to the table.

Metal legs, green Formica, scuffs, a few crayon marks—old and newish—made her feel as if the table had been there a very long time. The extension was in the middle and six quaint matching chairs were in place.

"How long is your lady friend going to be here, Uncle Brian?"

"I have to be at work this afternoon, so I should be heading home," she explained to Lauren, but looked at Brian, who raised an eyebrow and rested his head on his hand.

"After some pancakes, right?" Alicia set a stack in front of her. Big and fluffy with a dab of butter melting over the top.

"Go ahead. This is second breakfast for me," Brian said, or encouraged, or ordered. It was hard to tell. The man spoke with such authority, she was compelled to listen and wanted to follow his instructions. He was like a lifeguard even without water around.

"She likes 'em, Uncle Brian."

"I think you're right, baby girl. Her eyes just rolled back in her head for a second."

Lindsey completely understood why Lauren had spoken with her mouth full. The pancakes were wonderful and she wanted to let Alicia know as soon as they touched her taste buds. And the coffee was simple and excellent. She'd thought she was spoiled with Jeremy's one-cup flavored machine or the corner coffee shop at work. But there was something about the rustic flavor of black coffee that went with the pancakes and pure maple syrup.

"These really are great, Alicia. Thanks for going to the trouble." Lindsey stuffed another big bite between her lips. Totally in heaven.

"All I did was flip 'em. That paramedic sitting beside you learned some secret ingredient and won't give it up." Alicia pointed the spatula toward Brian. "He mixed up the batter and cooked breakfast before he caught some shut-eye."

If the screen door hadn't shut behind two men and startled her into silence, Lindsey probably would have blurted her astonishment at how kind this man had been to her. The men were close in size to Brian, but one was on a cane.

The other, once he removed his hat and wasn't backlit, she could tell was John, Brian's duplicate. "Woman of the house, two starving men need some lunch."

Alicia set the pancakes on the table in front of Brian. "As if one of them in the room wasn't enough."

"I was thinking that exact same thing." Lindsey watched John kiss and twirl his bride right back to the sink. The older man joined them at the table and a cup of coffee appeared at his fingertips. He had to be their father—they looked just like him. All three men took turns adding the same dollop of milk to their cups.

"Lindsey Cook, that jerk pawing my sister-in-law is my younger brother and this old man is my dad." Brian patted his dad's shoulder.

"Younger by twenty-three minutes but older by necessity, Scarface," John said.

"Let me see these stitches." His dad pulled Brian's face closer. "Alicia, I think you need to take a look at this mess."

"I'm done, Mommy," Lauren informed everyone, dropping her fork on an empty plate.

Alicia and John whispered softly behind her.

You're the only one left. You're the only one left.

The family voices teasing each other in playful exchanges swirled in her head. As everyone grew closer to the table the walls began closing in behind them. *Someone tried to kill me last night.* The pancakes turned to cardboard. She couldn't untangle what happened around her; it all mixed together just like when they brought Jeremy's body to shore. She could hear them, but she couldn't actually hear anything except a buzz in her ears.

"Lindsey, you okay?"

She whipped around and had to think twice about who had a hand on her shoulder. *Brian...murder you.* "I need out of here."

She shook off the help, the questioning concerns and just ran. The screen slammed behind her as she got her bearings and headed down the gravel drive. The second slam of the door let her know that someone was following her, but she didn't stop. She had to get free of everything.

Jeremy, his life, his dreams... If she disappeared, whoever was after her couldn't kill her. She could go back to her life on the beach, not worrying about responsibility.

"Lindsey! Where are you going?" Brian shouted.

"I can't stay here." She turned to face him but kept walking backward. Her shoes would be ruined from the gravel but she didn't care. She wouldn't need them on the Gulf beaches. Or maybe she'd try her hand up the East Coast. Get a job on a yacht or something. She had experience and knew some people.

"You can't walk back to Fort Worth, especially in those things."

"I'll call a cab."

He laughed. "Sweetheart, Aubrey doesn't have any cabs. Let's go back to the house."

"I can take care of myself. I don't know why I tracked you down last night." She must have been out of her mind. "And how do those people know who I am? Not one of them was curious about a strange woman in your bed. Do you pull this *danger* routine regularly?"

"For the record, the only female who's ever slept in my room happens to be five years old. Lauren took it over and I sleep on the couch when I'm home. That was Dad's room and I didn't know you'd get so upset—"

"I'm not upset. Why would I be upset? You claim someone's trying to kill me. What's to get upset about?"

"You're right. It's more like you're hysterical. I know a lot's happened to you since yesterday—"

He dashed forward and grabbed her arm before she could turn and run.

"Let me go." She twisted, flaying her arms.

"Ow, damn, that was my ear." His arms wrapped tighter, bringing her closer to his chest. "I'll let you go when you calm down."

Upset or desperate, she didn't know which, she just knew she needed to get free. She kept twisting. His arms tightened their hold. Soon her cheek was flattened against his cotton T-shirt. Grass and sunshine. His scent from working that morning should have put her off, but instead it attracted her like crazy. She tipped her head back, taking a long look.

He seemed relaxed. His jaw wasn't clenched, just sprinkled with a five-o'clock shadow. His chest expanded with normal breaths, as though the effort of chasing her hadn't been an effort at all. And he had the kindest brown eyes. Eyes that were easy to get lost in and forget exactly why she wanted him to release her. Eyes that cut through to her soul.

This man wouldn't have brought her to his family if he'd intended to harm her. Brian Sloane wasn't responsible for Jeremy's death or the car accident. He was helping her find the man trying to kill her. It was just that simple. Her overactive imagination screamed to a halt. Even if her racing attraction didn't.

Chapter Seven

If Brian didn't watch himself, he would be kissing the blonde in his arms and damn the consequences. Once he did, there'd be no turning back. He'd fall. Fast and hard and completely. Alicia waved from the kitchen door, verifying everything was all right. Last thing he needed was another lecture about getting involved with Lindsey Cook.

"Let. Me. Go."

"God…bless America. I'm too dang tired for this." He released his grip and the woman he'd like to devour fell into the tall Johnson grass between the fence and gravel.

Sitting on her backside, she drew her knees to the breasts that had so recently pressed against him. The urge to swing her back into his arms, jump in the truck and drive away from the pressures of job, ranch and family was right there. Obtainable, just a few steps away.

He couldn't leave. He was stuck here. His hands were hot resting on his thighs, itching to soothe Lindsey's back. It was the weirdest feeling ever, knowing so much about a person you didn't know at all.

"We're just trying to help." He finally forced words out. They weren't the words he wanted to say to her. Nothing close.

"I know. I'm…" she said with her forehead resting

on her kneecaps. "I'm sorry about the meltdown. I don't know what's happening to me."

"I'd normally say it doesn't matter, but I think it does." His ear was still ringing from the accidental slap he'd received on the side of his head. "What happened back there? Are you afraid of us?"

"No," she emphatically replied. "You wouldn't have brought me to your family if you intended to hurt me. And you aren't responsible for the accident last night or Jeremy's death. But the talking…the closeness of the kitchen…so many people. It just sort of all caved in on me and didn't make sense. I couldn't think or catch my breath."

He knelt beside her. "Are you thinking now? Breathing now?"

She looked at him, defiance and determination turning her eyes a deep, rich blue. The leaves from the oak trees lining their drive created a soft pattern of light and dark across her blond hair.

The sutures itched from the sweat popping out on his forehead. Desire pounded through his blood. The swiftness knocked the air from his lungs. He felt sucker-punched crazy. "What the hell's the matter with me?"

"What? I don't understand." The confusion brought her delicate eyebrows together.

"Nothing." He stood and extended a hand to help her to her feet, this time dreading the touch of her silky skin against his rough palms. He'd never given a second thought about blue eyes or corn-silk hair. Never. Thirty years old and he'd never had a notion to take a woman on a third date, let alone home to his family.

He could answer his own question, knowing what was the matter, even if he never admitted it to himself or to John. Especially John. The infatuated fool would be in hog heaven knowing he was riding the same love-sick bronco.

He released her hand as soon as she was on her feet. "You okay now? I don't have to worry about you trying to walk home, do I?"

"No. Not in these shoes. But for the record, you'll never catch me in a pair of those." She pointed to his scuffed-up, broken-in boots.

"Great. Let's go to the barn for some privacy." He shoved his hands into his pockets to keep from guiding her with a touch. He couldn't risk it, not until he got himself under control. "We're going to sit and talk like we should have last night at the Pan-Hop."

She walked next to him, silent, watching the ground.

"Do you have panic attacks often?"

Her head snapped around, her face full of question. "Never."

"You've had two in twelve hours." He propped the door open for ventilation. He was already hotter than blazes.

"How do you know they're panic attacks?"

"First off, I've seen a few professionally. And you have plenty of logical reasons to be upset."

"Is there any way to make them go away?" She sat on a bale of hay, legs and arms crossed.

He shook his head. "But you'll be okay. Promise." Stupid promise that he had no way of knowing how to keep.

"Why are you doing this, Brian?"

"You know why. I need to find out who framed my brother and me for murder."

"I get that part. I meant, why bring me here and involve your family? Why were none of them surprised I was here? And why do I get the feeling they aren't too happy about me showing up?"

He picked up and straightened tack someone had left on the rail. Delaying, but knowing he had to admit everything. She needed to know what was driving him and he needed to tell her.

"Finding information about your family has been a Sloane project for a couple of months now. I tried to tell you yesterday how we pieced everything together. And I guess they aren't too happy about more trouble on their doorstep."

"Because of Lauren's kidnapping and the court case deciding the future of her trust fund?" Lindsey scooted back and leaned on the post behind her, smiling. "I have a smartphone, too."

"Yeah, things are kind of up in the air about that. Any calls to the police or trouble around here, well, it might cause a judge to look unfavorably on my brother. He's trying to adopt Lauren."

"They want you on your best behavior and yet you contacted me anyway." Her lips tilted upward. "So you *have* been following me."

"Yes."

Lindsey's reaction wasn't what he expected. She tilted her head back, looked into the rafters and let out a long breath. The action eased his guilty conscience, but did nothing to ease his attraction. With her body arched backward, her breasts thrust upward. She did a little kick thingy with her feet slightly off the ground, and then she laughed.

Hoover Dam! He searched the barn entrance for work. Tack, salt, saddle, something heavy to lift and force his body into submission. Fifty-pound feed bags were ready to put in the storeroom. He hefted one on his shoulder and dragged another with his free hand.

There was something between him and Lindsey Cook.

Somehow, he knew it would be very good if he just gave it some time. That possible relationship—if he understood the use of that word—would go nowhere fast if he gave in to desire and crushed her body to his. What he wanted versus what he needed were fighting a battle, and he really didn't know which would win.

"Can I help?" Their hands collided on the edge of a feed bag.

"No." He hefted the bag to his shoulder and forced another under his arm. Work. Good, honest sweat would keep him on track. Head down, one foot in front of the other. Nothing to watch except his boots. "You should head back to the house."

"Not so fast, mister. I want some answers."

"I have work to do before I take you back to your rental." He stacked the feed and turned for the last bags.

"You agreed to tell me everything." She placed a searing hand on his chest.

"That's not a good idea right now." He looked at her hand, but it didn't move. Such a small thing that had him stuck in his tracks.

"We aren't leaving until you start spilling what you know."

"Drop it." He meant her hand. He'd tell her what he'd discovered. He just needed sleep and some space between them. Preferably an entire room, maybe filled with his family.

"I will not."

She pushed at his chest a little, nothing he couldn't have withstood, just enough to get closer and make him need to back up. But soon there was nothing behind him other than a stack of horse feed. She kept pushing and he sat, the bag he was carrying falling to his side. He went from looking at the part in her silky hair to staring up at her heaving breasts in a blouse that had no business in a barn.

Especially *his* barn.

"Okay, okay. You win." He threw his hands in the air, closing his eyes to block the view. Praying she'd back away with his surrender.

Silence blasted through him. The point of entry was her hand. No longer just a finger forcing his retreat. Her palm had weight behind it. He could hear her breathing hard, smell the maple-coffee scent of her warm puffs across his cheek. If he opened his eyes, he'd see her closer than she'd been since he'd carried her to bed this morning…. *If* he did that, there'd be no stopping his body from doing exactly what it wanted.

"Open your eyes," she whispered.

"Not a good idea." His body was about to betray his resolve and if she took a closer look…

"But you need to see this thing." Her breathy whisper was having an irrational affect on his senses.

"I don't think so."

No way they were talking about the same *thing*. But when she shook his shoulder, he opened one lid and then the other. Her look of iceberg fright was the complete opposite of his volcanic heat. He tilted his head, but his hat got in the way.

"Don't move. It'll get you."

By the look on her face it had to be a barn critter. "Is it a snake or a mouse?"

"Just be still and maybe it will slither away."

"Sometimes those things hang in the rafters until a mouse creeps by. You don't have to be afraid of—"

Lindsey's hand cut him off. Her stare moved behind his right shoulder and her body slowly inched on top of his. Within seconds she'd shifted and pulled herself onto his lap, and the simple rat snake disappeared under something in the corner.

"You can stand up now." And she should hurry up before he forgot what he wasn't doing in this small space with a gorgeous woman on his lap.

"But it's…"

"Hell's bells." He scooped her into his arms and marched into the sun before setting her on the ground.

When he let go, her arms were still locked around his neck and his arms steadied her at a tiny waist. Satiny red shirt to sweaty T-shirt. Slacks to jeans. Designer belt to rodeo buckle. City high heels stood on top of his country Western boots.

LINDSEY WAS COMPLETELY aware of standing on Brian's toes and pressing against every part of him. She didn't want to move. Safe from the snake and other horrible four-legged crawly things, she kept her arms where they were for a much simpler reason.

She liked Brian's hands where they were. Maybe it was the whole knight-in-shining-armor thing—even though she hadn't seen him near a white horse. But if her lips began moving, she'd babble nonsense and he'd never kiss her.

And, man alive, she wanted to know how he kissed. Bad, bad, bad idea.

Either way, she couldn't get higher or closer to him. He'd have to bring his chiseled chin down on his own. The smolder in his eyes she'd seen earlier when she'd run down the driveway returned and she knew what was next. His head tilted to his right ever so slightly, he bent his neck and then…

Tsunami tidal wave.

Brian Sloane was a skilled kisser. He had controlling

firm lips, just the right amount of curiosity mixed with pure desire. He applied the right amount of pressure on her back to tow her tighter against him without trapping her. She parted her lips and encouraged more exploration, doing a bit on her own.

He wrapped his arms tighter and raised her to his height. Her fingers had been itching to play with that hair growing at the back of his neck. His cowboy hat toppled to the ground.

Go for it. Encouraged by her body, she shifted and wrapped her legs securely around Brian's waist. He did some shifting of his own, including a move with his hands cupping her bottom.

"Uncle Brian?"

Lindsey's feet hit the hard dirt faster than she could blink her eyes open. Lauren stood holding Brian's hat, smiling and looking as though she knew something they didn't.

"Whatcha need, baby girl?"

Even though her heart was surfing faster than she'd ever surfed before, the little girl's cute giggle brought another type of smile to Lindsey's lips.

"Pawpaw said to give you back your hat 'cause…'cause your head was getting too hot."

"Thanks." He kissed his niece's cheek, shoved his hat on his head. "Now skedaddle back to your pawpaw."

Brian grabbed Lindsey's hand, forcing the rest of her to follow him back into the darkness of the barn, shutting the door behind them.

Desire skirted her like champagne bubbles popping up the side of a glass. More kisses? No. They couldn't. Brian dropped her hand and headed straight to the pile of leather, turned his back and untangled more rope.

"I think it was a very wise decision for your dad to

send Lauren outside. Don't you? I mean, your family's here and I've got a nut job trying to kill me."

"You're right. We're too different for this to work out."

"Oh, I wouldn't say that. My old self would be all over you for a beach romance." But they weren't at the beach. They were on a ranch. And someone wanted her dead.

"Old self? Beach romance?" He quirked one of those wing-tipped eyebrows.

He didn't need any more information about her. She was the one in the dark when it came to him and his reasons for helping her. She shimmied onto the bale of hay, just so no little creatures would crawl across her shoes. "Forget about me. Spill it. Where do we start looking for this monster who's been killing my family?"

"I've explained before that I'm a paramedic, not a bodyguard. Do I really have to tell you how I am not trained or skilled enough to investigate twenty-year-old murders?"

"You keep denying you're capable of looking for this guy. Yet you've discovered more than anyone else. I knew about my immediate family, but twenty years…? I don't understand how he hasn't been caught." She brushed aside a piece of hay that poked her backside and pulled her legs back tightly against her chest, keeping them far from the barn floor. "And by the way, I can hold my own."

"Right. That's why your feet have barely touched the ground since we've been inside." He waved toward her sitting position.

"Don't deviate from the question."

"Deviate? Son of a biscuit eater." He yanked a bridle or something to the dirt and the rest tumbled after. The tall man shifted his hat, blocking his eyes from her view.

He wasn't pleased. He mumbled a couple more disguised expletives, scooped up the tangled mess and started over.

"I can explain something I bet you don't even know."

"Is that right?" He looped a rope, finally free from the rest, into a coil and hung it on a post.

"I know all those 'sons of biscuit eaters' and 'Hoover Dams' are your attempt at not cursing in front of a five-year-old."

He acknowledged her with a *hmph* and a finger pushing the brim of his hat a little higher on his forehead.

"And I know why you brought me here."

"Why's that?" He looped a second rope over one palm, making it all nice and tidy.

"You hoped that if I met your family, I'd trust you and your information."

"Or it could have been I was tired, my head hurt and you were asleep in my truck."

"I don't think so. You wanted me to trust you and I think it worked." She could see the truth of her words reflected in his eyes. He had a hard glare when he was hiding emotion, but it was very easy to spot if you knew the signs. And she did.

"Got me all figured out?"

"You think you know me because you've done all that research and followed me around." She searched the shadows along the wall to verify they weren't moving, then she stood and leaped to the door. "There are so many things in my life that can't possibly appear on paper, Mr. Sloane. Aren't you just a wee bit curious?"

She backed out of the barn door, almost tripping on the way. She turned and squinted into the bright sunshine, raised her hand to shade her eyes and found herself face-to-chest with duplicate Brian.

"Back inside before they see you out here." John spun

her around and through the door. "We've got a visitor taking a close look at the property from the south."

"Why were you watching the road? Did you think we were followed?" Brian asked, moving quickly. He pulled keys from his pocket and went to a newish-looking locked cabinet. "How many and where?"

"Old habits are hard to break." John shrugged. "Same van parked across from Mabel's place now was in town three hours ago when I went to get the buttermilk. Binoculars or a camera lens reflected in the sun while I was trying to get a better look from the stock tank."

"Someone want to fill me in?" she asked. "I'm completely lost even though I hear English being spoken."

Brian and John removed weapons from the cabinet. They were a wonder to watch as they moved as one, without instructions, each anticipating where the other was reaching. They handed each other ammo and they both pocketed it, but left the guns empty.

"Whoever's after you found you." Brian connected a scope to a rifle on the edge of a stall.

"That's plain enough. What do I do?" Surprisingly, her voice hadn't quivered like her insides currently were.

"Sit tight," John and Brian answered together.

She swallowed the panic. Now that Brian had put a name to the overwhelming apprehension, it made it a little easier to handle.

"Just wait. Let us take a look," John continued as Brian slung the rifle across his back and climbed the ladder to the loft.

The horses, silent before except for a few shakes and tail flicks, whinnied or neighed—whatever the noise was that sounded so nervous. She could feel it, too. The tension from the two brothers radiated off them like sun reflecting on the white sand.

"I was hoping to avoid this for a while when I mustered out," John said, pushing the gun in the waistband of his jeans. "But someone insisted on sticking their nose into places—"

"Give it a rest, bro."

"See anything?" It wasn't the time for a sibling squabble. She didn't have a brother or sister, but she recognized the signs of an *I told you so* starting a fight. She'd had them often enough with Jeremy.

Now that her eyes had adjusted, she could see the tension in John's face and body movements. He was worried. His wife and daughter, along with his and Brian's father, were inside the house. All at risk because of her.

"I didn't mean to put your family in danger." She hoped she spoke softly enough that Brian couldn't hear her from the rafters.

John had been watching his brother but looked at her, quirking that identical brow in the same way that she adored on her cowboy knight. It didn't work. No magic tingling shot up her spine.

"But Brian did put them in danger, whether he meant to or not," he answered in a strong voice. Brian apparently overheard and responded with another *hmph*.

"Was that the reason you were upset this morning? I get it. Brian went against you guys and you think he chose me over his family."

"Are you through summarizing things you know nothing about?" He shook his head and looked away like she was entirely off base. Gone was the feeling of playfulness she'd had with Brian. With John, his intimidating looks made her feel inferior.

"Sorry."

For all the ways these two men were exactly the same on the outside, they couldn't be more different at their cores. Where John came across as commanding, Brian seemed helpful. Navy versus paramedic? Had their careers changed their basic personalities so much?

"You're part right, part wrong. It's more complicated than a two-minute conversation." John clapped a strong hand on her shoulder. "I'd feel better if you were in the tack room."

He'd pointed to the tiny closet with the snake. "There? No way."

He mumbled real curse words and stomped to the bottom of the ladder. "Got anything?"

"Plate's blocked. One guy. Camera. Don't see a gun." Brian stuck his head over the edge. "Lindsey confused me with a reporter yesterday. Any chance this could be one?"

"Give me your shirt and hat. Then you can find out." John loaded his handgun while Brian practically jumped from the loft.

Both men tugged their T-shirts over their heads. John's sunglasses slipped to the ground, Brian picked them up. Identical muscles rippled as they pulled the borrowed shirt over their heads, changing identities. Brian tucked his in like John had looked before undressing. His brother left his out, hiding the weapon at his waist.

An untrained man shouldn't confront a potential killer. "You can't send him out there. Aren't you the Navy SEAL?"

"Was. Now I'm a rancher, just like him." He jerked his thumb toward Brian.

"I can handle myself."

"You keep saying you're just a paramedic," she argued. Brian handed his brother his hat and she saw the teasing smile. "What's so funny?"

"Nothing. I'm just glad you finally believe me. Don't worry. I'll be fine."

"I don't believe you're doing this. Why not call the police?" Lindsey wanted to kick off her shoes in spite of the creepy crawlies and run with him.

"John." Brian ripped the white bandage off his forehead and stuck out his hand. "Keys?"

The twin now dressed like Brian dangled his car keys above his brother's palm. "Don't do anything stupid like follow him and wreck my car."

"Alicia's car."

"Community property state." John flipped the handgun, handle to Brian. "Be careful."

Brian checked the weapon, nodded and stuck it in his waistband.

"Will someone tell me why we don't call the police and report a trespasser?" If something happened to Brian, it would be her fault for convincing him to help her. "I get the feeling this is more complicated than Lauren's adoption."

"That's a long story, Lindsey. John can explain while I'm gone. Don't forget…he may look like me, but John's a married man." He kissed her lips in a brief flyby and headed out the door.

She stared after him in a stupor, not really knowing how to feel. She'd been so confident she was breaking through that tough exterior just a few moments ago. And their kiss—whew. The heat of it still had her insides all gooey.

Chapter Eight

"Come on, Lindsey." John spoke in a calm voice, but those tense lines were still straining his good looks. "Let's take a look out in the paddock and give our paparazzi a show. Remember to stay between me and the house. If he does have a gun, he'll never get a clean shot."

"What? Do you think he's going to shoot at us?"

"I don't think that's his M.O. From what I've seen, he seems like a guy who likes to plan things with a little more control of the outcome."

The roar of a muscle car coming to life and driving too fast up the gravel made John cringe and shake his head. He seemed so much older than his brother. Older and more experienced.

The duplicate of the hand she loved curved around her waist, touched her back and guided her around the metal fence. John was just as handsome as his brother but strangely, she felt nothing. No pings or tingles of excitement. Only frightened worry about Brian.

The Sloane house was far enough off the road, you could barely hear a car drive by. Even a muscle car with a muffler as load as Manhattan.

Screeching tires. Then a shove to her knees kept her from turning to see the cars on the road.

"Damn it, Brian. I told you not to go after him," John shouted, slapping his thigh as he stood straight.

"I take it he didn't listen to you?"

"Never does." He stepped a little farther away from her now that he wasn't playing Brian for the man in the van. "Let's head inside."

"Aren't you going after him?"

"In what? Brian's truck? That thing belonged to our granddad. There's no way I'd ever catch them."

"Then you should call the police."

"Yeah, about that. The police won't be stopping Brian Slone, they'll be stopping John Sloane, who will probably say I'm running off more reporters."

"You'll explain that in a slightly less cryptic way once we're inside?" She was totally lost. They had a problem with reporters, too? The questions about why the police wouldn't help spun her around harder than a wipeout in Malibu.

"Sure."

They sat at the table again and Alicia joined them. The plastic wrap was removed from Lindsey's pancakes and they were popped in the old microwave, which took up a third of the kitchen counter.

"Mrs. Cook was the coolest teacher in school," John began. "She let our class hang out on her property. We had plenty of fires there in a pit her husband had used at one time. Nothing ever happened until the night she died."

Alicia laced her fingers through her husband's. "My guy here," she patted his hand, "was about to leave for the Navy and we were arguing about what would happen. He was upset, fought with Brian and they both stormed off. They didn't speak for twelve years."

"Back then we shared the truck and always left the

keys in it. I needed some time so I spent the night alone. Brian came back to the Cooks' place in the morning. But witnesses saw our truck leaving the actual fire."

"It wasn't stolen?" she asked. "And neither of you left in it?"

"That's right. For twelve years I thought Brian drove it home and he thought it was me. You see, it was our responsibility to put the fire out that night. It spread to the barn where they found Mrs. Cook—"

"My second cousin."

"Everyone thought she tried to put the fire out and the barn collapsed on her. She had massive head injuries." Alicia continued the story. "Brian took the blame for the accident. He didn't want anything to stop John from getting into the Navy."

"He said he did it, even though he thought you were responsible for it spreading?" This morning, the brothers had moved together as though they'd never been apart. What must it have been like back then when they hadn't been separated for twelve years? "Wait, that still doesn't explain why the police won't help him."

"This town blamed Brian for Mrs. Cook's death and treated him like a convicted felon even though it was ruled an accident," Alicia explained, while John's knuckles turned white in a death grip. "He lost a full scholarship to college and each time something goes wrong in town, the cops blame him."

"Like for Lauren's kidnapping? I did some research of my own."

"They arrested him, then tried to beat a confession out of him before he made it to the jail." John's look turned to steel. He might say he was a rancher, but the man in that chair was every inch a Navy SEAL. "He still hasn't told me how many times it happened over the years."

"Too many," Alicia whispered.

"But he's a paramedic, he helps save lives."

"No one knew that except Alicia and Dad. Everyone else thought he was a drug dealer."

"You aren't serious?" She couldn't believe it. That shy cowboy/paramedic? "How could anyone get that impression from that teasing smile of his? I've known one or two— Sorry, but he's definitely not into drugs."

"We know that, but he never cared what the town thought and wouldn't let us set them straight," Alicia said.

"Why does he want to find the murderer so badly?" A shiver shot up her spine. "It's still hard for me to believe someone really wants me to die."

"He's been obsessed with clearing our name since we cleared the air."

Alicia jabbed his shoulder. "Since I threatened you both if you didn't speak to each other."

"I was wondering why he'd go to all the trouble to help me, especially after the police didn't give his theory any merit." She toed off her shoes, dreading having to walk on gravel in them again. "So what now? Will he come back soon?"

"Those shoes are a disaster waiting to happen," Brian said behind her, then pulled the door open. "I go chasing bad guys and you can't keep a sharp eye on things? I've been standing out there for five minutes. Some Navy SEAL."

"Give me some credit. I heard the car pull in. Maybe you needed to hear how ridiculous it is for you to continue this investigation."

"I caught up with the photographer in the van. He said he got a tip there might be a story. He snapped a few pictures." He looked at his brother. "You know what that means."

"What does it mean?" Lindsey asked, looking around the room.

"We should go." Brian latched on to her upper arm.

"Don't be silly," Alicia said. "The way the sheriff watches the ranch, this is probably the safest place for you both."

"Yeah, it's better if you take off before more show up. Or someone we don't spot gets too close." John was really talking about the murderer.

"I can't believe you're agreeing with him, John." Alicia was clearly upset.

"It's okay, everybody. I need to head to work at three." She gently removed her arm from Brian's grip.

"You aren't going to work. Too much exposure. My family's at risk now and I'm sticking to you until we figure this thing out."

"But I—"

It was useless to defend her point of view. He'd made up his mind, and left the room.

"John, you can't let him just take off," Alicia pleaded with her husband.

Lindsey could see that they needed privacy. There wasn't much space to give them in the tiny house, but she went into the living room.

An older man raised a finger to his lips. Lauren was asleep on his lap.

"I'm JW and you must be Lindsey. You'll be safe with him," he said in a low voice. "He's got reason to be broody, but don't let him be. I think you'll be good for him."

"I beg your pardon?"

He grinned. It was a window to the future on how his two sons would look at his age. Still handsome and charming. "I'm the one who sent Lauren out earlier."

The heat of embarrassment spread up the back of her neck. First, Brian's father had seen that hot kiss, and second, he already had them as a couple. "It was just the intensity of the moment."

"You might call me a dirty old man for spying on you. But I'm not and wasn't. I just happened to look. And you two were kissing where anyone could see. Including the man in the van." He lifted his chin toward the hall bedrooms. "He knows that. The man who's after you. He'll assume you're with Brian now."

"So I really have put everyone in danger. I'm so sorry."

"Not your fault, Lindsey. That madman started the feud with my family twelve years ago. I just wish I was strong enough to come with you."

Brian filled one doorway with a bag over his shoulder. John filled the other with Alicia ducking under his arm and snuggling against his side.

"We'll keep looking into the records, trying to make sense of the deaths," JW said.

"Ready?" Brian asked.

"You should get a cheap phone. Same as during the kidnapping, we talk through Mabel. Don't underestimate this guy. He's got a lot of practice and he's patient."

JW moved Lauren to the couch and stood. The little girl was in a deep sleep. Brian hugged his dad with one arm, very manly, then bent to kiss his niece, very sweetly. Alicia hugged him and opened her arms, hugging Lindsey before she could react. John just tapped her shoulder, pressed his lips into a straight line and nodded.

"Got plenty of ammo? Any idea where you're headed?" John asked. "Never mind, we don't need to know."

"You take care of each other. And don't forget to eat. I think we forgot to eat for three days. Hiding out isn't easy, but sometimes it's necessary." Alicia looked up at her husband, who winked.

"You'd better take the car," John mumbled, but his reluctance was evident.

If she wasn't mistaken, there was a story behind that car. She envied the family dynamic between these people. Their courage through Lauren's kidnapping was unmistakable. There might be strain between the brothers, but they were trying to make it work.

"It'll be at the airport when we pick up a rental," Brian said, making an executive decision.

"I should call Beth and let her know I won't be at work." Alicia handed her a cell and she dialed.

"Keep your head down, boy-o."

"You don't have to tell me twice, sir."

Brian gathered a few things while she lied and left Beth a message that she wasn't feeling well.

No one followed them out. She slipped her feet into the heels, following Brian to the trunk of the cherry-red Camaro. He threw his bag inside along with the rifle she'd seen him with earlier. She watched him retrieve her purse from his truck. He gallantly opened the muscle car door to let her in.

"You okay?" he asked, tossing his hat in the back.

She wasn't sure she could answer him clearly.

"Are you certain about leaving with me? I'm far from certain you're doing the right thing. In fact, I'm not sure I understand what it is we're actually doing."

He kissed her over the window. Crisp, clean, on the lips as if he'd been doing it for years. And she kissed him back the same way. Wanting more, knowing there would be more.

"Are you going to tell me what we're doing?"

"We're going to catch this son of a bitch."

Chapter Nine

Entering his office, he turned on the recorder before he talked himself out of documenting his mistake the night before with the car and again when Lindsey had run to Brian for help. He'd already gone through the pros and cons of admitting he'd underestimated his opponent. And now he had a new one—Brian. It seemed the twin cowboys were slightly more complex than he'd given them credit for.

"What made you expose yourself to— Strike that. Expose is the wrong word. I became too inquisitive and forgot the key to my success—patience. The real question is how Brian Sloane could make me forget my protocol."

That answer needed pondering. The leather of the couch creaked under him as he stretched out.

"Side note. Brian Sloane is certainly good-looking. Many would say he's handsome, especially in his work jeans and T-shirt, but he would never succumb to my... indulgences. He'd never beg for his life. Perhaps that's why he's higher on my radar than Lindsey."

He sat straight, realizing he'd recorded the wild, un-controlled side of his personality. The half he rewarded, not the disciplined planner he wanted the world to have firsthand knowledge about. He could rerecord that particular segment—just run it backward and tape over it again. It was almost cheating.

"And I hate cheaters."

The selected words he left here were for history. He didn't need to *cheat* by deleting the tape. Just clarify.

"That's what's so frustratingly brilliant about the Sloane brothers. Facing two of them is almost like they're cheating. I watched Brian while he was with my next victim. He's very attached to her. Even through the camera I could see his attachment growing."

He smiled at his play on words. Then eyed his decanter, longing for the sharp sting of the liquor washing down his throat.

"Brian's feelings for the Cook girl will eventually work against him." The vodka decanter caught his eye again and he swung his legs off the couch, sitting closer to the clear ambrosia.

"When John turned from their drive, I knew he would pursue me. Very predictable, since I would have done the same thing. And that's what I'll enjoy most about this last campaign. Those brothers will force me to be more creative in my thinking. I must also be careful and not misjudge them again. This game is different. They think they know something about me."

He picked up the vodka decanter and tipped two fingers' worth into his glass.

"They think I'm patient and predictable, waiting for an opportunity to strike. No one understands me, nor will they. The best time for me to strike is soon and unexpectedly. Catch her off guard and blame the Sloanes, just like I did twelve years ago."

He turned the recorder off, then swirled his drink and

saluted the hidden microphone in the ceiling. Knowing he had to finish his reward sooner than he'd wanted.

"They'll never see me coming."

Chapter Ten

Brian drove the speed limit, not taking any chances about being pulled over. This wasn't the time to push his luck with law enforcement. His one saving grace through the past eight years had been his boss at the ambulance company. He'd looked at him as a person and given him a chance when no one else would after a background check.

Playing the part of a supposed criminal had been rebellious for a while, but when he needed money to supplement the ranch, there'd been nowhere to go. An EMT course at a junior college and the trust of one man willing to hire him showed him a different path. He'd advanced as a paramedic in Fort Worth but had never cleared up that bad-boy image his hometown had accepted.

"I really hope you know what you're doing," Lindsey mumbled again. She'd been doubting him from the moment he'd pulled out of his drive and stated they were headed to her house.

It was clear as a hot summer's day that he didn't know what he was doing. When would she catch on? How was he supposed to find a man who had orchestrated fatal accidents for fourteen people and never been caught?

"You know, Lindsey, I'm a rancher or a paramedic, depending on what day you choose. I can track a bobcat or keep you alive with a rig full of equipment. But keeping you safe from a murdering madman? I think that needs some special training."

"As in police?"

"You got it."

"Then why are we headed to Jeremy's?" she asked, maybe picking up on his hesitation to pull into the drive-way. "What are you looking for?"

"We'll take a quick look at your cousin's papers and hopefully find a place for the police to begin an investigation. If the cops have evidence, they'll have to get involved and offer you protection."

"Are you certain you want to go back there?"

He shook his head. "We need your cousin's papers and you need clothes. And sensible shoes."

"I have hiking boots and running shoes."

"Get them." He backed into the driveway. "Can I park in the garage?"

"Sure, the opener's in my purse. Give me just a sec."

What was he doing? Was she in danger here? Was he so desperate to find a clue that he hadn't thought about her safety? He was out of his depth and needed to convince her. He couldn't protect her. He shouldn't be trying to. He'd been forced to get Lindsey away from his family and that was as far as he'd thought about it.

What if the rat bastard chasing her took his vengeance out on Lauren? That couldn't happen. They'd been through enough with the little girl's kidnapping and Alicia's crazy stepfamily.

"Here it is." She pointed and clicked before he could say wait.

Garage was empty, not even a lawnmower. And there probably wasn't anyone in the house, but he needed to make certain.

"Why don't you get behind the wheel and I'll go inside

to check things out. Alone. Just in case, be ready to get out of here in a hurry."

"Sorry to disappoint, but I'm not staying anywhere by myself. That'll be my scared-to-death hand hanging on to your back belt loop as you search the creepy dark rooms." She got out of the car. "My door is staying open for a fast getaway. You should leave yours open, too."

He began to shut the Camaro's door, but left it open after a cute, manicured finger pointed directions to do so. He'd laugh if she weren't so serious. Then again, being cautious couldn't hurt. He unlocked the trunk and retrieved his SIG. Gun in one hand and keys in the other, he unlocked the dead bolt.

A gentle tug on his pants assured him Lindsey was just behind, hanging on tight. He cracked the door open, listened, slid through the opening and flipped on the lights. Total silence in the house with the exception of the gurgling fish tank. They made a thorough search, room by room. They flattened curtains to the wall, opened closets filled with her cousin's things.

It was midafternoon. The curtains and blinds were closed in the main bedroom, making the room darker, but nothing was blacked out. But even if it had been, he recognized the smell of death. In his line of work he experienced it often. The distinct smell of blood hit his nose as soon as he cracked open the door.

"Go wait in the kitchen."

"Why?" she whispered, death grip still on his jeans.

"I don't think you should see this."

"I stay with you. Period."

"Shut your eyes and cover your mouth. Whatever's in there…don't scream and have the whole neighborhood calling 911."

She did as he instructed. One glance at the body on the

bed and he knew the person was dead. Between the smell and the amount of blood on the white sheets, there wasn't any doubt. It was recent; most of the blood hadn't dried.

Lindsey moved to his side, released his jeans, and he knew what was next. He wanted to scream along with her. Or shout and curse the animal who had done this. The sound began behind him, but he was able to shut it down by blocking her view and placing his hand over her open mouth.

The light from the master bath was a beacon in the dimness. He shoved Lindsey through the door and she immediately knelt by the toilet, heaving. He left her there.

There was even less afternoon light with the door pulled closed. He used the back of his hand to flip the light switch. Eight years as a paramedic and he'd never seen anything that turned his stomach. This did. He hadn't noticed it in the dim light, but now that his eyes were adjusting, the blood was everywhere.

Some of the blood spatters on the wall were dry. Could the murderer have done part of this after they'd left? Had he been here waiting for Lindsey to come home after the accident?

If he had dropped her off at the curb last night, that would have been Lindsey.

The woman was bound to the headboard, her blistered hands limp. It looked as if she'd been forced to hold a searing iron. Brutally tortured. There were dozens of slashes and burns on her body. She'd been in a lot of pain for hours.

Checking for a pulse would be useless, but the paramedic in him had to be certain. There was no way to get near the body without stepping in her blood. He reached the head of the bed and raised the blood-soaked throw pillow by its corner.

The fright in the woman's eyes—he'd never seen anything like it. Patches of her face had been skinned. He couldn't imagine what type of psycho would do something like this. He touched her carotid artery.

Dead, but not yet cold.

The victim had pale blond hair, sky-blue eyes—she could easily have been mistaken for Lindsey. But the man chasing the last of the Cook family knew her. Had studied her. Wouldn't make the mistake of killing someone in error.

No, he'd done this deliberately to make it look like Lindsey was dead.

"Oh. My. God. Oh, my God." Lindsey stood in the bath doorway. "Brian, how could anyone do this? She doesn't have— There's nothing left— Didn't anyone hear her scream? Didn't she scream? There's so much blood. How could someone do this to another human being?"

Dropping the pillow, he leaped away from the bed, spinning Lindsey away from the horrific scene and slamming the thin door behind him. Lindsey's breathing became erratic. She shook, her hands flailing and hitting his shoulders.

"Look at *me,* Lindsey. You are not having an attack. Not now. Do you hear me? We don't have time for you to fall apart. Get control. You're hyperventilating and we need to slow your breathing."

Her panicked eyes locked with his as he slipped his hand over her mouth, allowing her to draw air through his fingers. He slowly laced his fingers of his free hand with hers while her breathing slowed. He needed her to hold it together.

"You okay?" he whispered, swallowing down the bile gathering in his throat and wanting to forget everything he'd seen in the bedroom. "Do you know her?"

She shook her head, eyes still wide with disbelief.

"You said you had a pair of hiking boots?"

She nodded.

"Grab 'em, along with some jeans, T-shirts, a coat. Anything you might need. You aren't coming back here."

She drew a deep breath. "We should— What about the police? We can't just leave without—"

"Yes, we can. I've been picked up too many times over the past twelve years. They're going to lock me up *now* and clear me *later*." He looked at the blood he'd tracked onto the tile. "If I'm lucky."

"That's ridiculous. We can prove you had nothing to do with her death. The…the photographer. He knows you were at the ranch this morning."

"I didn't get the guy's name. There's a bunch of circumstantial evidence pointing toward me." He'd researched her family, tailed her, confronted her at the sandwich shop. Then the accident and witnesses who saw them leaving the hospital together. "Damn, how could I be so stupid? The man trying to kill you is smart. He's been following you, yet you haven't seen him. Hell, *I* followed you and didn't see him."

"What are you talking about?"

"The van. Seeing the van parked so obviously on the road directly in front of the barn. He wanted us to see him, to feel threatened and leave the ranch. That was his plan. This girl hasn't been dead long. It's a setup to get me out of his hair. While I'm in jail, he'll eliminate the last Cook."

Lindsey's face went pale under her golden tan. "That's despicable. I can't imagine anyone going to that much trouble to kill someone. You can't know that for certain."

"Right or wrong, we don't have much time." He gently walked her back a couple of steps to crack the door open behind him. "I have a feeling the killer will phone in an anonymous tip, bringing the police here shortly."

"That's ridiculous. I've been with you the whole time. Or your family was right there."

"And during the time you're proving all that, who's going to be protecting you?"

"The police, for one."

"They won't. You'll be alone. Vulnerable to attack."

"What if I'm with someone? You can take me to Beth's house or Craig's. I can hide there with his wife." She shoved her hair back from her face. "No, that would put his family at risk and Beth lives alone. They'd all be in danger."

"That's why we leave. Together."

"All right. But I'm not going back into that room to get my stuff."

"I'll take care of it. Did Jeremy have a laptop?"

"It's in his study, mine's in the living room."

"I'll get you a couple of days of clothes. Where's a suitcase?"

"In the hall closet. Brian…" Her soft touch down his bare arm stopped him. "I'm sorry for getting you involved."

He pulled her to his chest, speaking into her hair. "You aren't to blame. The psychopath targeting your family is the only person responsible."

"But what about your job, your family? I can disappear and not worry about this guy again." She tilted her head back. Her soft blue eyes were filled with fright and questions. "You don't have to do this."

The idea of her walking out of his life forever made his brain scream no. If she really wanted to leave, he'd go with her. But would this guy walk away, too?

"Whoever's trying to kill you has been at this for almost twenty years. Do you think he'll give up? Ever? After seeing what he did in that room, I don't think he's going to stop with you. He likes it." Saying the words left a disgusting taste in his mouth, but he knew they were true. "We have to stop this guy."

"You're right." She dropped her forehead against his chest again.

Keeping his arm around her, he placed a towel across the counter, very aware of every minute they delayed. "Put what you need on the towel. And grab stuff for a first-aid kit."

She slipped from his arm and was done in seconds.

"Trust me, Lindsey." She nodded and he placed a second towel loosely around her face to block the view and smell, then walked her back to the living room. "Did your cousin have any legal papers? Anything that might help us figure out what this guy is after?"

"I'll find them."

"We're out of here in five. If—"

"No ifs. I'll get everything from his office and be ready."

He left her and went back to the murdered woman, hating to disturb the scene even more, but he had to. He couldn't wipe this place clean just in case the killer had left evidence. But the police would find out who Brian was fast enough. His prints were in the system, not only because of his job. The police in Aubrey had booked him when he'd confessed the night of Gillian Cook's death.

He typed a detailed text to his brother and took a minute waiting for the reply, deleting the phone history afterward. Then he composed a message to an officer he knew in Fort Worth and left it on the screen, leaving his phone on the dresser in plain sight. He hoped the cops would find the man in the message and he'd give a word in Brian's favor.

The phone was useless since the GPS could ping their location as soon as he turned it on. His brother knew where to meet him. That message would be retrieved, but the police would be delayed ordering the phone records. He didn't need much time at the apartment. A couple of hours of rest and a plan. That was all.

They wouldn't be able to show their faces in public, so he grabbed the things on top of the towel and shoved clothes from her dresser inside the carry-on and turned off the lights.

Lindsey was scrubbing her hands at the kitchen sink, a laptop bag next to her feet. There was something wrong with her actions. The rubbing got faster, almost frantic. She was in shock.

Lindsey was certain blood was on her hands. How it got there, she didn't know. She hadn't touched the dead woman, but it was there. The afternoon sun was bright coming through the kitchen window, and her hands were covered in soap as she used the scrubber to claw at her fingers. But she could feel the cold blood sticking to her skin.

Brian's warm exhale skimmed her neck, and his fingers wrapped around hers under the scalding water before he reached around her and cut the faucet off. "It's okay, Lindsey. We should leave now."

He put the strap of the bag over his shoulder and nudged her toward the garage door.

"Wait. We'll need food." She pulled cans and frozen dinners and health bars and dropped them into grocery sacks.

"We should go—"

"Stop. We need this." She dropped everything that wouldn't spoil into a sack.

Brian backed away and carried the bags to the back of the car without another word of protest. There was a small ice chest in the bottom of the pantry and she dumped ice inside for the milk and orange juice along with the six-pack of beer and bottle of wine that had sat in the back of the fridge since Jeremy's death. The freezer door shut and she was eye to eye with a picture of her and her cousin. She jerked it from under the magnet and shoved it in her bra.

Brian lifted the cooler and guided her to the car.

"Wait! There's bottled water still here from Jeremy's funeral. It's behind the door."

"I'll get it."

Lindsey buckled up and looked at the picture of her cousin. The weight of the water being added to the trunk shifted the car a little, but all she could do was stare at Jeremy's image. *Now what?*

"One more thing." Brian sat in the driver's seat. "Take the battery out of your phone and put it in the glove box."

She did as he asked. "How are we supposed to run from a man capable of the butchery inside the house?"

"First thing we're going to do is head to my place and get some sleep."

"Sleep? There's no way. How can we go back to the ranch?"

"I share an apartment in Fort Worth with several of the other paramedics. They switched us to twelve hours on and twelve off, so my partner, me and four others from the firehouse went in on a place to sleep—and only sleep. It's cheap and my name's not on the lease. My partner's taking the day off since I'm on mandatory leave and it's the beginning of the others' shifts. We'll have the place to ourselves."

"You've got this all figured out, then."

"Hardly."

"Wait!" She stopped his hand before turning the ignition. "Jeremy had a fire safe for important papers in his bedroom."

"Stay put and I'll get it."

Lindsey tried to wait once Brian was back inside the house. She hadn't told him the safe was on the shelf and hadn't given him the combination.

He could find it. She could handle five minutes by herself.

Five minutes crept by. Then six. She entered the kitchen, expecting him to laugh at her silliness.

The house was empty. Still...it felt as if the walls were shaking. Impossible. It must be her insides.

Brian had been right. Now that she knew about the panic attacks, she could recognize the signs and try to prevent them. She peeked around the door. A creepy feeling hit her, like watching a scary movie where you knew someone was about to die. Creepier still...the shaking couldn't be her imagination. Impossible. It must be her insides. She took a deep, deep breath and let it out slowly.

No shaking. No panic.

Entering the hallway, she ran her fingers along the wall to guide her. Something hit the other side...in her bedroom. "Brian?"

"Lindsey! Run!"

Chapter Eleven

The body slams, crashes and sounds of a fight grew louder as Lindsey ran straight to Brian's voice. The dresser overturned, the mirror smashed in front of her at the door. She flipped the lights on. Glass and small objects had been knocked from the dresser and mixed with the blood on the bed.

Worrying about the dead woman's body struck her as a bit bizarre. She watched a man dressed in a black jumpsuit wait for Brian's attack near the closet. Brian swung, connected with the man's ribs, spinning him sideways. But the man in black countered by slamming the back of Brian's thigh, forcing his knee to the carpet.

Then the man in black lifted something shiny from the floor.

"He has a knife!"

"Get out of here, Lindsey!" Brian shouted between defensive grunts. "Now!"

Trying to help Brian didn't make a lot of sense. She should run, but couldn't. If no one heard the woman scream, they wouldn't hear her either. He needed professional help—the police. Her phone was in the car. Frightened for them both, she released her grip on the door frame and turned. The bedsprings creaked and time slowed.

It was as though each second was recorded in her mind with an exclamation point. The creak made her look behind her.

The man leaped across the bed, stepping on the poor woman's legs. His arm stretched toward her.

Two more steps and her body lurched in reverse, back into the bedroom. He jerked her hair, yanking while she screamed. She lost her footing, slamming to the floor. He was over her, the knife raised.

Even his eyes were distorted with thick, shaded glasses. The knife descended, she threw her hand up to deflect. Pain. Her own hiss and scream blocked out all the other sound. Where was Brian?

A deep shout, more of rage than warning, and the man in black disappeared from her view.

She rolled to her stomach and blinked away the automatic wetness in her eyes. The knife shot against the door, bouncing past her into the hall. The man kicked the side of Brian's knee sending him to the floor. He jumped over her, scooped up his knife and ran.

"You okay?" Brian asked, pursuing him through the door.

"Catch him," she gritted through her teeth.

Brian's running steps vibrated the wood floor where she rested her cheek and sucked a few painful breaths through her teeth. She crawled to her feet, staggered to the hall bath, got a hand towel for her arm and locked the door.

If Brian didn't return… *He will.*

The door shook with the pounding. "Lindsey!"

She trembled so badly it was hard to turn the knob to let him inside. Should she? Was he alone? Was there a knife to his throat forcing him to call out to her?

"He's gone, honey. I saw him drive away. You all right?"

"I'm…I'm fine." She twisted the knob and lurched backward as Brian stumbled into her. She tried to get past him. "Let's get out of here."

"That bastard cut you?"

"Let's look at it later." She turned her injured arm away from him, trying to shove the rock in front of her aside. "Did he hurt you?"

Brian used his calming gaze and gently prodded her to the sink. Looking into his face and feeling his soothing touch made her think everything would be okay.

"You're going to need sutures. I'll get the wound cleaned a bit, then get you to an E.R." He turned the water on, ready to clean her cut. "This is going to hurt."

"Later." She jerked her arm to her side, blood oozing from the gash. He reached for her arm again and she turned from him, reapplying the towel. She moved away from his comforting arms. "No doctors. Please, just get me out of here."

"We do this now, Lindsey, or I drive you straight to the hospital."

Didn't he know he was covered in blood? Was it his or the dead woman's? She was beginning to gag at the thought.

"Please take that shirt off. Jeremy's clothes are still in his room. I'll rinse my arm while you get rid of it."

From the corner of her eye she watched him in the mirror as he shoved away from the counter and jerked the T-shirt over his head. "I need to take care of this now."

She closed her eyes. "Please change."

She heard the running stride of his boots, then they disappeared on carpet.

Before she lost her courage, she quickly forced her arm under the running water, gritting her teeth in agony as the sink turned red below her. Queasy and surprised she hadn't pulled out all her hair, she got a clean towel and put it on her arm.

Brian reappeared in a tight-fitting T-shirt Jeremy had worn all the time. "Got first-aid tape?"

"Maybe in the cabinet behind me."

He looked at the wound, pulled the sides together and replaced the towel. "The closest hospital is on I-20. I can get us there in eight or nine minutes. They'll take good care of you."

"I'm staying with you."

"That gash is deep enough to need sutures," he said as he dropped the tape on the counter.

"You did your own."

"But—"

"You said this killer won't stop until I'm dead. All the reasons we weren't going to the police still apply." She tapped her finger against his chest. She knew he agreed with her when his brows drew into as straight a line as his lips. "I'm sticking with you until we catch this son of a bitch."

Chapter Twelve

"Choose a bed, Goldilocks." Brian set her suitcase down next to the bathroom and tugged her cousin's shirt over his head.

Wicked-tight jeans drew her attention to his bare lower back and then up to his sculpted shoulder blades. He put water on to boil. She was either completely woozy from the cut and car ride or the attraction was growing so strong she couldn't stop thinking of running her fingers over his strong shoulders again.

Then he faced her and she noticed the tint of his skin was pink from the blood-soaked shirt he'd left at Jeremy's.

"I'll get my sewing kit." His long stride took him into the bedroom faster than she had time to react.

She knew what the water and kit were for. Cleaning her arm and his scrapes. There would be no complaints from her. Complaints would land her dropped off at an emergency room. The last thing she wanted was to be separated from this man she'd come to trust so quickly.

Convincing the authorities she was in danger would be very difficult without evidence. This murderer couldn't be infallible. Somewhere, at some time, he had to have made a mistake. And she was going to find it.

"You weren't kidding about beds and nothing else," she said, loud enough he could hear her in the bedroom. With a stiff upper lip, she peeled off the packing tape Brian had used to hold the towel in place. She tried not to dislodge the towel, afraid it would start bleeding. If it hadn't stopped, Brian swore they'd be on their way to the hospital.

"Kick your high heels off and get comfy," he said from behind the closed door.

The place was tiny but open. There was a futon on one wall folded as a couch, with the sheets folded on the end. She sat facing the television, leaning back to get rid of the wooziness in her stomach.

"This place is surprisingly clean. Are you sure it's six men sharing? I expected a lot worse."

"Yeah. Six males, but I'll admit that one of the guys pays Debbi—she lives down the hall—to pick up, do the dishes and the laundry."

"Now the cleanliness makes sense." She had the tape off by the time Brian returned without the pink-stained chest.

"I pick up after myself," he said, swiping his chest dry. "I do let her wash my towels and sheets since we all share them."

She closed her eyes, unable to watch as he peeled back the makeshift bandage. He wore gloves, and had gauze pads ready to replace the dish towel on her forearm.

"You ready?" he asked with a steady voice.

She nodded, her mouth suddenly dry, silently praying it wasn't as deep as he'd thought. But behind her closed lids, she fell onto a carpeted hallway, a man with bottle glasses and a large knife headed for her. She jumped when Brian touched her arm.

"You drifted a minute. I'm ready to give this a shot. Are you certain?"

"It was just the gloves. They reminded me of the attack."

Brian's finger touched her chin, coaxing her to look into his rich brown eyes. "This is really going to hurt, Lindsey."

"Is this normal practice for paramedics? To scare their patients before beginning?" His eyes soothed her as much as the gentle touch he had through his gloved fingers. "Did you learn how to stitch people up in paramedic school?"

"Taught myself for the horses. Cheaper than a vet coming out when one of 'em got sliced." He went into the kitchen.

"You mean—"

"Drink this." He set a tea glass full of her favorite deep, dark merlot onto the side table.

"If I consume all that on an empty, woozy stomach, I'll be drunk. I may even throw up."

"Something important for me to remember—the lady can't hold her liquor." He sat on a chair he'd brought from the card table in the kitchen. "I'm serious. I need you relaxed. I can't deaden it and it'll hurt worse if you're jerking your arm."

When he picked up the needle and wet thread, she picked up the wine, squeezed her eyes shut and guzzled. She concentrated on a picture of his jeans and tapered waist. The muscles in his back. The picture of him was so vibrant there was actually a catch in her breathing.

"Don't worry. I know what I'm doing," he soothed.

Her imagination didn't prepare her for the level of pain that a tiny needle created when punched under her skin. But his voice assured her through everything he did, every step of the way, no surprises. Once he was done, she saw six neat stitches before he covered her entire upper arm with a bandage."

"Think you have enough tape?" she asked remembering some of the images she'd concentrated on of him in those tight-fitting jeans. She'd drunk the wine much too fast and was definitely tipsy.

"If you won't let me take you to the hospital for antibiotics or… Yeah, you're keeping the bandage. First sign of infection and there won't be any talking me out of a real doctor. Got it?"

"I agree. No arguing." She carefully formed her words so they wouldn't slur. "Thanks for doing…well, for everything, Brian."

She'd been a flirt since the second grade and Ronnie Willhite had told her she was pretty and wanted to kiss her. She wanted to crawl onto Brian's lap, wrap her arms around his neck and kiss him until his vision was as blurred as hers. But she slumped back against the cushion instead.

One short nod and he put away his equipment. "Showers and then some shut-eye, unless you feel like eating."

The thought of food made her head swim. "I don't know how you expect to sleep while that murdering serial killer is still out there."

"I plan on relaxing and closing my eyes."

"But—" He handed her a second glass of wine.

"I can't drink that. The room's already spinning."

"Good. You need some shut-eye." He set the glass on the table next to her.

When he smiled, she wanted to forget everything except the kiss they'd shared that morning. She wanted to be back in front of the barn with her legs wrapped tight around his waist. Or maybe sitting on his lap again, even with a snake slithering in the corner. It beat having a serial killer slither free outside their door.

"We can't stay here. It can't possibly be safe."

"We weren't followed, and a former Navy SEAL and former Marine will be outside watching the place very shortly."

"You forgot to explain."

"I sent a message to my brother. He got in touch with one of his buddies. We'll get some rest, and as soon as the cops show up at the ranch, he'll take the Camaro home, leaving us Mabel's sedan. For the moment, we're safe enough for you to get some rest. You're going to need it."

She lifted the glass and he clanked it, following a salute with his beer bottle. He walked to the window covered in thick black curtains, lifting the edge to take a look at the street below.

"A Marine and a SEAL?"

"That's right. John's calling a buddy. One'll be out front and the other 'round back. That should make you feel safer than a police squad car. Mac's already here." He disappeared into the bedroom, continuing his explanation. "He'll have a phone for us. If you want on the Net, codes are taped to the side of the TV. Bolt this thing behind me. Or you could fall asleep. I've got a key."

He ran out the door, pulling a T-shirt on, hiding the handgun stuffed in his pants, and she was alone. She should be upset that he'd made the arrangements without telling her. Or maybe she wasn't because she was relaxed enough not to care. Either way, she would not be falling asleep anytime soon.

Not even with guards to protect her and being slightly drunk. But she could begin searching Jeremy's laptop and powered it up. Most everything she did on the internet for the past four months had been on her phone. She'd lost most of her web clients after her cousin's death because she'd been dealing with his affairs and getting into the habit of working somewhere every day again.

Now she was glad she hadn't given away any of her cousin's things. Even his clothes hung in his closet. It was time to give it all to charity. The idea of being so alone no one else would want anything you left behind made her so sad. But there wasn't anyone left.

She was alone.

All because of a horrible man targeting their entire family. "Why? Why us?" The laptop didn't power up correctly. It was trying to open nonexistent files on a memory stick Jeremy had left plugged in. She removed it and dropped it back in the bag. When everything was booted and signed on, she skimmed one file, then another. Brian walked in, moved the merlot closer to her fingertips and she sipped.

"Should I tell someone I won't be coming into work tomorrow?" She sipped again, the merlot warming her shakes away. "Beth will probably stop by Jeremy's after work tonight to see if I'm okay."

"They might get a call before they close. Homicide arrived at your house shortly after we left."

"How would they know where I work?"

"Paystubs? Did you ever sell a phone to a neighbor? Anybody around there know where you work?" He walked to the window again.

"Oh, I guess they do. It's more likely that they remember Jeremy managed that store."

"That's good." Then back to the kitchen, where he put some of the food she'd taken from the house into the refrigerator.

"Oh, my gosh. You want the police to think that dead woman is me?"

"For a couple of days. Long enough to find out why this guy wants you dead. He's obsessed with your family. There has to be a reason."

She set the laptop on the futon and quickly stood. She probably would have fallen straight off her high heels she'd been wearing all day. She was shaky even on bare feet. "Brian, did that woman look a lot like me?"

He encircled her within his arms and she knew the answer before he said, "Yes."

"That's the reason he did those things to her face?"

He nodded, holding her tighter. "He also burned her fingerprints away."

"That's horrible. She died because of me. How can I live with that? No one else can die, Brian." Her fingers curled into a ball around his shirt. "Who's to say my life was worth more than hers?"

"Me, for one. Not more, but just as important. And I think your cousin would want you to live." He kissed her forehead, keeping her safe in his embrace.

"You don't know me." She tilted her face to look at him.

"Then that's something we'll have to change."

Brian delivered a trail of hot kisses down the side of her face. His short, practical fingernails gently gathered her hair as his lips continued a path back up to her forehead. Lindsey turned her mouth into his path, and the fireworks were as explosive as the kiss earlier that morning.

Their tongues danced and explored. His fingers barely grazed her waist and then she felt a tug on both sides of her shirt. Brian backed away, leaving her lips cold and desperate for more of him.

"As much as I'd like to keep on with this—" he dropped another kiss on her cheek "—I'm dead on my feet and heading to bed." He stood and stretched his arms high, raising his shirt to expose an inch of his flat belly. "And no, that's not an invitation, unless you want to curl up in my arms. Our first time is not going to be when we could be interrupted at any moment by my brother."

She stood there with her mouth open at the audacity of his words. *Our first time?* If she hadn't agreed with him, she'd be insulted at his assumption. But she was super attracted to him and wanted to explore more of those abs she'd caught a glimpse of.

There was something about the way he took everything in stride. She'd seen the horror on his face at finding the dead woman. He couldn't hide it as much as he tried. But he didn't allow it to override his ability to think on his feet and come up with a safe place for them to go.

"A Marine and a SEAL. Sounds like the title of a book."

Books!

Jeremy had been reading a book in Cozumel. She opened the link to his electronic library. There were lots of mysteries, thrillers and action books. Then she found the one that had stuck out—*Texas Real Estate and Land Titles.* Why would her cousin be reading this heavy material on vacation? It had to be connected.

But how? She reached for another sip of merlot and realized the glass was empty. She should get some water before she was seriously tipsy. The apartment spun as she stood to fill her glass. She barely made it back to the futon and definitely couldn't do anything with the clean sheets. She'd laugh and giggle but was too busy yawning.

Laptop closed, sheets used as a pillow, she curled on the mattress with her back secure against the cushion.

She drifted off thinking of how well Brian's hands fit around her bottom.

If they'd only met before all this...

SOMEBODY HAD TIED one on before coming to the apartment to sleep. Brian banged on the wall between his bed and the front room. "Come on, guys. I'll remember this the next time I come in and you're getting some shut-eye."

A few seconds was all it took to remember he was here only with Lindsey. The thrashing continued. SIG palmed, he was barefoot and shirtless at the door to the other room. He stuck his head around the frame, staying low like his brother had reminded him.

A nightmare. Lindsey was alone and fighting only someone in her dream. The loose sheets were in knots at her feet. Her red silk shirt was tangled high under her breasts, showing him a flat, tanned stomach. He returned his weapon under his mattress and noted that he'd been asleep a couple of hours.

Lifting his blue-eyed dream into his arms, he cradled her, shushing her nightmare like he would have Lauren. He placed her in his bed, then gathered her stuff, bringing it all to his room and locking the door. If any of his roommates did venture past Mac in the hallway, they wouldn't barge into his room.

The vent blew right on his bed. That was the way he liked it. But Lindsey was already shivering. He pulled the covers around her and had every intention of being a gentleman. He'd stay on his side of the bed, not touching or exploring or...anything.

He did manage to lie on his back and not move. Completely prepared to hit the hay again. Yep, that was his intention. He could do it.

Right until Lindsey curled tighter, sidling up to him.

He lifted his arm and she molded herself to his chest. Shifting to his side was more comfortable, then they were spooning. He couldn't very well keep his arm above his head and get any sleep. Was it his fault if it wrapped around her middle?

Sleeping—really sleeping—with a woman wasn't something he was used to, because he never did it. There was no reason to. He didn't bring women here and certainly didn't bring them home to the room next to his father's.

Sleeping at the moment wasn't happening either. He was too aware of the soft breasts pressing on his arm. Enjoying the rise and fall of her chest, the silkiness of her hair against his chest. Everything about her made him want her and yet made him want to wait until the time was perfect.

Finding a murder victim in your house—not to mention in your bed—was repulsive enough. Running from the murderer probably didn't make you very amorous either.

Yet, he was wide-awake and only thinking of making love to the woman in his arms. He should be thinking about a plan. Since he wasn't sleeping, he should go down and talk with his brother.

That was the last thing he wanted to do, but he eased away. By the time he sat on the second bed to pull on his boots, Lindsey was tossing as though she was in another bad dream.

Making sure Lindsey got some rest was as important as figuring out a plan of action. He didn't want her to fall apart or have more panic attacks. His boots were soundless falling back onto the carpet. He slipped in beside Lindsey before he could change his mind.

Resting on his elbow, he traced her troubled brows,

smoothing them like his mother had after his nightmares. A rhythmic motion that he'd always thought hypnotic. Her jerking slowed, then stopped, and she relaxed into his side.

John had already outlined a plan and could tell him details later. Differences aside, he'd be the good, inexperienced brother and salute when told what to do in order to save Lindsey and his family.

It would be the only time John would get that level of cooperation from him. To keep the woman in his arms sleeping soundly, he slipped an arm under her head and the other around her tiny waist. Even with his eyes closed, he could see her sky-blue eyes sparkling like diamonds in the sunlight.

Diamonds in the sunlight? What the heck? He wasn't a poet and had never thought like this about any woman. Hell, he'd never thought like that before, period.

Chapter Thirteen

"I'm in blessed shape and health for a man of my age. I will, however, admit that fighting a younger paramedic proved tiring."

The wall panel hiding his souvenirs and recording equipment slid open. He placed the bag with the clothes he'd worn during the fight with Brian Sloane along with the rest. All neatly labeled and vacuum sealed to preserve the DNA.

"I should remind curious minds that I have no desire to be blamed for crimes I did not commit, nor will I be denied the accomplishment of one either. It will be hard for authorities to believe my flawless record. I have kept the necessary proof of each and it is properly organized." He pushed the button, closing the panel behind his wall safe, then shut the doors to the actual safe and replaced the heavy books on the shelf, hiding the catch.

"What an exhilarating day. The police believe Lindsey has been killed, and now Sloane is wanted for her murder. Yes, quite an accomplishment. I will have to work late into the night making up for what landed on my desk today, but it is well worth the time I spent."

Time for his vodka. Then the work that paid his bills.

"Sloane acted exactly as predicted. Until the time that the police place him in jail, it will give me the necessary interval to plan the next stage of my Cook finale. I dare-say I hate to postpone the preparations for the hunt." He toasted himself, letting the vodka heat his throat. "And the kill."

Chapter Fourteen

"She doesn't deserve nightmares." Brian had tried to explain to his brother several times about his fascination with Lindsey. He barely understood it himself, so the words he'd stubbornly uttered over the past month sounded like a lovesick cow speaking a foreign language. Today was no different.

"I'm sure there are other people who can handle that problem." John pushed a piece of notebook paper across the card table. "My plan is the only way to be safe. I've written everything down for you. I'd like your word that you'll follow my instructions."

John, the man with all the answers, casually tipped his chair back against the wall and linked his fingers behind his head, waiting. Brian knew that look. He'd had one himself years ago when he was confident and certain his way was the only way. Before life got complicated with possibilities.

Walking away from the ranch or from years of paramedic training. Losing his heritage or starting a new life. His dad and John thought they knew his answer. Hell, he didn't even know his answer, so how could they? He reread the list.

Number one in big red caps: Brian surrenders to police. Two: Lindsey secretly travels to a friend's house—

alone. He glanced through the ways to avoid getting noticed. And the last thing on his brother's instructions: let the police find the murderer.

"You want me to sit around and do nothing? Did that work for you?" With a flip of his wrist, Brian sent the list back across the table. "I've already given my word and I won't go back on it. You might as well understand that I'm not going to salute you like one of your soldiers. You can't order me to retreat into a jail cell and wait for this all to blow over."

The Naval Lieutenant inside his brother didn't get it. Brian wasn't leaving Lindsey's side. Not voluntarily. Not until she was safe and had choices for her safety.

John ignored the paper as it floated to the floor. "You can't be serious."

"As serious as you when you were wanted for murder a couple of months ago and kidnapped Lauren to keep her safe."

"That was different, Brian. You don't know the first thing about this woman."

"You didn't know Alicia after being gone for twelve years, yet you jumped in when she was in trouble." He scrubbed his face with his hands, trying to think, and ended up irritating the sutures on his forehead. His brother's look hadn't changed. If anything, he was more irritated with the mention of his wife. "Come on, John. I need you to back me up here."

"I've trained for rescue missions. We had a plan and were lucky it worked."

"You know your instructions are a death sentence for Lindsey. We have to find this guy. If we run now, he'll disappear again and kill her later."

"There's no choice here, bro. We can't do anything

with your name and our mug shot on every television screen in the state."

"That didn't stop you from helping Alicia."

John stood, knocking his folding chair to the floor. "Damn it, why won't you listen to me? Every cop in Dallas–Fort Worth is out for your blood. The P.D.'s catching all sorts of flak for not taking her reported threat seriously."

"Good."

"Not good. They don't want explanations, they want your head on a media-frenzied platter. And she's not even dead."

Brian tapped the table, trying to think. He wanted to understand and accept his brother's advice. But shouldn't his brother understand why he wanted to help Lindsey? John hadn't ever been supportive of him finding the truth behind Mrs. Cook's death. Saying things like "what good would come of it" and that "they all knew the truth so why did finding whoever was responsible matter?"

Well, it mattered to Brian. He was the one who had been blamed for her death. Not John. Not his father. And not the murderer.

"Even if I did follow your suggestion, Lindsey won't leave town. Not without me."

"You don't know that. You haven't asked her." John stood at parade rest.

The way he thought he knew everything they should do now, and how they should act, ticked Brian off. It was his breaking point. He slapped the table, prepared to brawl to win this argument. "This dictator role you've taken on needs to stop. Just accept the fact that we're not running. It's done. Now, explain what you would be looking for on the laptop and we'll do it. Lindsey used to run a website company. I bet she could—"

"Finding hidden files has nothing to do with design. You're over your head trying to rescue your new girlfriend and can't see that you're both drowning." John kicked at the cheap chair. "I told Alicia you'd be an idiot about this."

He put a lid on the feeling of self-pity and screwed the lid on tight. He was the one who chose to take the blame for the accidental fire. Not John. Not anybody. If he'd trusted his brother back then, twelve silent years could have been avoided. He wasn't going to cause a rift between them again.

"Hey, stop shouting. I hear fine and Lindsey's still in there sleeping. I know we'll need to find a safe place to lay low until the police eliminate me as a suspect. What I don't know is why you're so reluctant to help."

"The news is reporting her murder and you're the primary suspect. Unless the police talk to her, know that she's alive, how are they going to eliminate you other than with a bullet between your eyes? They will find you, Brian. Then what?" John asked. Genuine concern or authority oozed out his military straightness. He hadn't answered Brian's question of what was holding him back.

"It'll be okay. I have a solid alibi."

"That's right, he does," Lindsey said from the bedroom door behind him. "Don't you need to be at home talking with the cops, John? I mean, you're part of his alibi, too. Can't you tell them that poor woman isn't me?"

"Right. Like they'll believe me."

"You doing okay, Lindsey?" Brian watched his brother's spine straighten even more with Lindsey's presence. She looked as if she'd been dragged through the wringer. Her hair was prettily tangled from the tossing and turning she'd done even while she'd been safe in his arms. Her eyes were slightly puffy with smudges of mascara. He wondered if she'd taken a look in the mirror or avoided it, afraid of what she'd see.

"Just peachy." She grimaced as she folded her arms across her chest. "I found a memory stick last night. It might mean something."

Brian remained at the table, willing his brother to leave. He didn't want to argue any longer, just wrap his arms around Lindsey and maybe take off to hide in the mountains.

"What happened to your arm?" John asked. His brother was calm enough on the surface, but Brian could see his tolerance chipping away.

Right then, he didn't feel like the older, responsible twin at all. He tried to catch Lindsey's eye before she filled John in on the details he'd left out about their encounter with the murderer. Luck wasn't on his side.

"A maniac sliced it with a knife after he murdered an innocent woman in Jeremy's house. A woman who looked just like me, apparently."

Apparently she didn't like him holding back information either. It was Brian's turn to stand suddenly and let his chair collapse with a clang to the floor. The noise didn't slow John or Lindsey's discussion.

"You heard the authorities think you're dead?" She nodded and John's eyes narrowed. "My brother neglected to mention you'd been wounded. Did you see a doctor?"

"It was a minor altercation." Brian tried to play it down. An identical set of jaws clenched, and fingers formed fists. Maybe they'd get that brawl in after all.

"Brian stitched it up last night." Lindsey lightly stroked the overkill bandage he'd wrapped over the sutures. "I will never doubt the power of a deadener again."

"Are you nuts, man? She needs a real doctor, a hospital, antibiotics."

Lindsey shook her head and compressed her gorgeous lips into a straight line. "Let's get past this, John. You've argued too long and need to admit that you've lost this battle. I'm following Brian's lead regarding this matter. If you can't help, then you should go."

As tall as his blonde beauty was, she still had to tilt her chin to meet his eyes. But there was nothing weak or confused about her glare at his brother. She wasn't bluffing. She'd made a decision and that was the end of the discussion.

John placed his chair back at the table and mumbled about stubborn women and idiot brothers as he sat. There was a new energy and assuredness to Lindsey's step as she crossed the room, scooped up John's list and opened her cousin's laptop. Brian watched, leaning on the kitchen wall, completely confused as to why he suddenly felt proud.

"How long before we need to leave?" Lindsey's nails gently clicked keys while she raised one blond brow in question.

"Soon," he said, along with his brother.

"Did either of you hear me when I said there was a memory stick with Jeremy's laptop? I should show you what I found last night before Brian got me drunk."

"Drunk?"

Brian pointed to his upper arm and mouthed *stitches* to his brother.

"I remembered something strange from my last trip with Jeremy." Lindsey ignored his brother. "I teased him because he was reading a Texas real estate manual, even highlighting passages. Who reads that sort of book *after* you buy a house? Anyway, it's still on here."

"It's a start. Is there any other file that might be unusual?" he asked, not needing his twin's challenging glare. He knew nothing about computers. He rode horses or in an ambulance. Neither allowed a lot of time for gaining computer skills.

"I'm not sure, but the drive indicates there's a lot of data there. I can't find a file list. It looks as though Jeremy just used a hidden file program. You can get them off the internet. The trick will be thinking of his password."

"I have friends who can take care of that." John had a shoulder against the wall, listening, a hand rubbing the stubble on his chin.

"I can figure it out. Jeremy was like my brother. I knew him pretty well."

Brian looked up to see the same "yeah, right" look on his brother's face. Lindsey harrumphed.

"The concept might be foreign to the two of you, but I did know Jeremy. Thanks for the offer, but these are my files now and I'm keeping them." She shook her head looking back at her keyboard. "The protection program he used was just a GUI."

"Did you say gooey?" John asked.

"Yes, a Graphical User Interface that's easy to install and use."

"I think Lindsey speaks your lingo, bro." Brian crossed his arms and leaned back in his chair, striking the same pose his brother had earlier.

"Can I see you for a moment?" John asked.

He stood, and the first thought that raced through his head was what would break when they came to blows in the bedroom. Nothing important or nothing at all. He'd successfully controlled his temper for twelve years. He even avoided the teens around Aubrey who didn't know why their parents were angry at him. They just liked to pit their fighting ability against the town's bad boy. John was the only person who got under his skin far enough to get a rise.

His brother turned, and they were face-to-face. Once again, it was like looking in a mirror. Gritted jaws. Clenched fists. Narrowed eyes. John moved and instinctively Brian brought up his hands to defend himself.

"Damn it, Brian. I don't want to fight you." John clapped a hand on his shoulder. "After I leave, I can't help you. You won't be able to come home. It'll be more than the local police camped out on our doorstep and it won't be safe."

Brian jerked away from his brother, feeling more alone than he had in the twelve years they were apart. "Don't worry. I wouldn't put you guys in danger. I'll keep my distance and keep you out of this mess."

"You're taking this all wrong. I didn't mean it like that." John scrubbed his face, then his head, the worry apparent in his eyes. "I was thinking it might be easier if we switched. You stay at the ranch and I'll protect Lindsey."

"I thought that wasn't possible with my new scar?"

"Don't be too hasty and hear me out. I have special skills and training that might come in handy."

"I think I can hold my own. We're not much different."

"With most things, sure." Both of John's hands went to the top of Brian's shoulders. It was the closest they'd gotten to a brotherly hug since they'd graduated from high school. "You know this guy's not going to stop. What are you going to do when you find him?"

Be more prepared than the last time. His hand went to the gun at his waist.

"Are you prepared to pull that trigger and kill someone?"

"If it comes to that." He didn't have to debate it. The

answer was clear in his head and heart. He'd defend Lindsey without question.

"You could both die." His brother sounded more like his father for a minute.

He understood wanting to protect his twin. It was exactly the reason he'd stepped forward and taken the blame all those years ago. "It means a lot that you want to take my place, but this is something I have to do."

His brother clapped him on the shoulder, squeezed his fingers. "I figured. I've seen the way you look at her. I didn't think you'd do anything different, so I got Mac to let you use his place for a few days so you could lie low."

AFTER THE SLOANE men headed to the bedroom, Lindsey had been tempted to follow them and eavesdrop at the door. But only for a second. If the thin walls didn't allow her to overhear an argument, just like it had earlier, she'd ask Brian what John had to say later.

The brothers were identical in so many ways, and yet different in so many, too. John acted so confident, but she had a sneaky suspicion he was just worried about losing his brother. Brian had appeared so withdrawn at first. It was much easier to like him when he was around his family. Whether he realized it or not, he smiled more on the ranch. Maybe it was the youthful playfulness even when he argued with his brother about serious subjects. Or maybe he was just cute. Period.

Right now she needed to find a lead. Some tiny bit of information to begin a search. There had to be something.

The slash on her arm ached. If she rubbed it or complained, Brian would insist she go to the hospital. He'd be arrested and she'd have no one to help her find this madman or a connection to her family. If the police hadn't found a reason to investigate any of their deaths before, why would they now?

"Lindsey have you seen my folder with your family information?" Brian began thumbing through Jeremy's papers.

"Hmm?"

"I had the folder last night at your place when you noticed the fish food had moved," he said, looking at her. "Then I— Son of a biscuit eater, I left it on the coffee table."

She went through the picture of her living room in her head. "It wasn't there this afternoon when we went through the house."

"He knows exactly what we know." John walked to the window, taking a quick look through the blinds.

"How can he use that against us?" she asked. "Isn't it more important to concentrate on why he's killing my family?"

"What if he doesn't need a reason and he's just a nut job? How are you going to stop him then?" John asked.

John was right. The murderer was patient and had outsmarted them twice already. All he had to do was wait until the police stopped investigating him. Then one day when she was alone, he'd resurface and finish the job, crossing her off whatever insane death list he had stuffed somewhere.

"You okay? You look woozy and didn't answer."

"Maybe she needs the hospital after all. Mac will take her."

"I'm fine, and I'll decide if I need to see a doctor." The nausea she felt had nothing to do with her arm. It was from being scared down to her bone marrow at the idea of being hunted for the rest of her life. Hunted and never knowing why.

"You sure you're okay?" Brian asked. "The police wanted a motive. If we find the reason why the murderer has a feud with your family, we'll find him."

John looked at his watch. "I need to hit the road and would feel better if you got going."

"He's right, Lindsey. We need to head out. Mac gave us the keys to his place for a couple of days while we come up with a plan."

"There's got to be something to this book and memory stick. It's just going to take me time to piece it together." She shut the laptop, then held her hand out to John. "I'm so sorry I've brought more chaos into your family, but I'm so grateful I'm not facing it alone."

"It's more as though we brought a killer to your doorstep." John pulled her into a bear hug. "Don't let him do anything foolish," he whispered.

"I'll try not to."

John nodded toward his brother. They both paused, and he left.

"Are you absolutely certain that we're doing the right thing? Your brother seems very upset at the idea of us trying to catch the killer." She shoved the laptop in its case and slung the strap over her shoulder. "Shoot, I'm upset about finding a murderer."

"Sometimes he forgets who's saved his hide more than once. But if you have any doubts about my abilities—"

"No. It's nothing like that." Maybe she trusted too easily, but she did trust him. He'd put everything on the line for her, a virtual stranger.

With her bag of clothes over his shoulder, his hands warmed her inside and out when he slid them along her back to draw her closer. He smoothed her hair behind her ear and trailed his fingers across her now-flushed cheek.

"I'll do my best to keep this guy away from you, Lindsey. I promise."

"I believe you." She thought she spoke, maybe a broken, breathy sentence. But it didn't matter.

Brian tilted his head and leaned close. Her hand felt the wild cadence of his heart under the thin cotton of his T-shirt, along with the strong muscle tone. He oozed protection and sexiness. As his lips claimed hers, she remembered the feel of her legs wrapping around him, how he'd lifted her with ease and how she wanted to repeat the wild forgetfulness from earlier that morning.

Gentle, firm, in control. He was all those things. She wanted more, wanted to drop their bags, kick off their shoes and head back to his room. Who was she kidding? She wanted his arms tight around her and didn't care if they moved another inch.

His lips gently pulled away, replaced by his finger smoothing the fire-parched surface.

"It's a good thing my brother was in here for the past hour. Otherwise—" he touched his lips to her ear "—I might have kissed you when you woke up and taken you straight back to bed."

She gulped, wishing they'd met last week when she'd first noticed him in the coffee shop. She dragged her nail across his lips, avoiding his teeth when he tried to snag it. "That's pretty presumptuous, considering we just met yesterday and you haven't even bought me dinner yet."

"We'll get that taken care of as soon as the police aren't trying to arrest me for your murder."

"Absolutely, cowboy. It's a date."

Chapter Fifteen

They were in another unremarkable four-door car that belonged to the woman across the street from Brian's family. The car couldn't be traced back to them, but she still turned her face away from drivers pulling alongside. Lindsey had picked up enough at the ranch to understand that JW Sloane was spending his nights at Mabel's and she was practically family.

It had been a long while since her family had consisted of more than Jeremy. And she was ashamed to admit that she'd put him off several times before begging him to come to Cozumel with her. He'd gotten his life together and she'd kept "bumming around," as he'd put it.

"You sounded pretty knowledgeable with all that computer lingo back there. I guess I should hire you to get a website together for the ranch."

"I let all that go when I moved here."

"Aren't you good at it?"

Brian's question seemed like ordinary conversation and probably was. She was half mad at herself for walking away from that dream. She'd been getting new sites and had loyal customers. It was hard to explain to an outsider that one of the last conversations she'd had with Jeremy was about keeping her word and responsibility.

"I hold my own."

"Then why'd you give it up to sell mobile phones?"

She'd promised Jeremy that Cozumel would be her last "fling." She hadn't meant it at the time, knowing full well that she'd talk him into another spur-of-the-moment vacation later. But when he'd died, it all rushed her as though she'd been hit by the lip of a wave and totally wiped out. She hadn't surfed since.

"Why are you riding around in an ambulance instead of on a horse?"

"Touché. So you know how to surf?"

"I practically lived on the water. I surfed every day I could." The rush and power of doing something well hit her as strong as the desire to run back to the ocean. Leave searching for the serial killer to someone else trained to find a sicko like that. Leave and disappear on the beaches with some waves and a good board.

"Wow. Not sure I'd like it out there with sharks under my toes."

"I loved it at the time."

"Is there any money in web design?" Brian drove, seeming as though nothing was wrong. Not as if they'd seen the killer or were running from the cops. He was so laid-back she could easily imagine him as a surfer. No bumps in a wave for him.

The conversation was such that two people might have on their first date. She knew so little about him other than he was a rancher who supplemented his income by working as a paramedic.

"I suppose there's money in it for those who try. I mainly did it for friends. I couldn't spend much time on it while at work. There wasn't good internet access at the beach huts."

He rubbed his forehead, scratching the stitches on his wrinkled, confused brow.

"Most of my jobs revolved around renting boogie boards to tourists. I'd follow the coast, working in different cities, crashing with different friends—or a friend of a friend. Sunup to sundown. Barefoot with sand between my toes. Spring break until it was too cold to open the rental huts. I made enough helping with websites to pay my share of the rent when the beaches were closed. That's all I cared about."

"You sound like you miss it."

"I shouldn't. There was no stability in that line of work. And I'd never get ahead, as Jeremy constantly reminded me. Wouldn't you know that as soon as I have my act together, a serial killer smashes my car trying to murder me." A cracked laugh escaped from high in her throat, making her sound a bit frazzled. Or a little loony.

Brian cleared his throat, creating a nervous silence that she didn't know how to get herself out of. There was nothing to comment on except the darkness. In the middle of nowhere, on the edge of civilization, but far enough away to remind her just how much light streetlamps provided. Brian slowed for a stop sign and her heart jumped into her throat.

It had only been twenty-four hours since her car had been hit. There weren't any other headlights, but her hands gripped the edge of her seat, bracing herself. A warm hand covered hers. His strength shot a different type of adrenaline through her system.

"It's okay."

His deep baritone voice whispered a complex comfort in its simplicity. Something her body understood more than her mind. His calloused fingertips rubbed her cold hand back to life. She no longer concentrated on the crash. The excitement of his kiss washed over her and she wanted to recapture all the exhilaration she'd felt moments before leaving his apartment.

The dashboard lights softened the sharp angles of his face and smile. He waggled his eyebrows before he looked both ways along the deserted road and stepped on the gas again. Bringing her hand to the side of his thigh, he laced his fingers through hers and held tight. So did she.

"Mac's place should be around one or two more curves," he said after a couple of minutes.

"Have you been there before?"

"I never heard of the guy until my brother texted me. I am, however, great with directions. I never got lost when I drove the ambulance."

It was on the tip of her tongue to ask if they should trust a man they didn't know, but it wasn't necessary. Mac had already proved his friendship to them both by guarding the door while they slept. She also wanted to avoid speaking of the reason they needed to hide. She was enjoying the silence and holding Brian's hand.

Two days ago, if Beth had told her those two things would be appealing, she would have fallen over laughing. Now having this man's thumb tenderly caress her hand was sweet and sexy at the same time.

The stress of the past day had kept her adrenaline at extreme levels. There was a strong desire to forget all of it for the rest of the night. Just being on an even, relaxed keel was appealing. But not as appealing as being safe enough to explore every inch of the man beside her.

The thought of how they could fill some downtime had her blood bubbling with excitement and tingling so much, her body shivered.

"I know you want to plan out our next move. So do

I. Let's find Mac's place and then we can work our way through Jeremy's paperwork."

"Sure." She didn't want to think about papers or trails or clues. But most of all, she didn't want Brian to let go. And she didn't want to think about why.

How could she consider an interlude—to put it nicely—with a guy she just met yesterday?

Impossible. No way. That was the old Lindsey. The Lindsey who tossed her sleeping bag on a beach chair half the summer. She was responsible now and couldn't do things like that. She wouldn't sleep with Brian Sloane, no matter how much she wanted to. No matter how tempting or how safe she felt with the man trying to save her life. She would not break her promise to Jeremy.

"Here we go." Brian used both hands to turn the big car onto a dirt road overgrown with tree limbs in spite of the drought they'd seen all summer. "Mabel's going to have a cow if these sticks scratch her paint job."

"Uh-huh." She stuck her hands under her legs to keep them from wandering back to Brian's.

Less than a minute of driving and the tree limbs stopped creeping near the car and then were gone. Camouflage for the Marine's home that was at the end of the short road. What had seemed like a dark trail actually opened onto a large open field surrounding the small house.

"You okay?"

"I'm fine, and you can stop asking me that."

He parked the car in back, off the driveway and close to the back door. He twisted in his seat, no longer looking casual, but very calculated as if he was thinking about how each word would sound before they crossed his lips. "If you're upset about what I said earlier, I can apologize."

"I don't need an apology." And hated that he thought

she did. "I need something to let me know that I'll eventually wake up from this nightmare."

JUST HIS LUCK. Hold a girl's hand and she calls it a nightmare.

Brian knew it wasn't him and could admit he had no business telling her earlier he'd rather take her to bed. Crass. Rude. Ungentlemanly. And a couple of other things if his daddy found out. Being nearly thirty years old wouldn't stop the old man from giving him a good earful on how to treat a lady.

"One day the nightmare will be over." He hoped. "Remember, we're going to catch—"

"This creep." She laughed, finishing his sentence. She dropped the partial braid she'd been nervously plaiting and slapped her jean-covered thighs. "I think that must be our mantra for this adventure."

"And a damn good one to remember until we do." Brian laughed. Easy, pleasant and infectious. "Adventure, huh? Ready to find out if Mac has running water and electricity?"

"Where are we?" she asked as they unloaded and unlocked the door.

"A little north of Fort Worth. Not too far out in the boonies."

"It feels like the boonies. I'm horrible at directions, but it doesn't seem possible that we're still near Fort Worth."

"We're not far. Straight highway and we can be back at your place in half an hour. Good, he has lights."

"You were just joking about the running water, right? I never did get that shower."

"Try that door." He pointed to one next to the small kitchen.

She cracked the door enough for him to see a sink,

gave him a thumbs-up and disappeared behind the closed—and locked—door.

Mac's house was totally off anyone's radar if they were looking for someplace Lindsey would be hiding. She'd be safe here, which was Brian's primary objective. He heard the shower and a long, relieved sigh through the thin wall. He finished unloading the food from Mabel's car, breaking a sweat and making the skin under his bandage itch.

But that wasn't all that was itching. His skin was irritated by the T-shirt as he put away the last of the beer and wine. He was irritated at himself when he realized he was looking for an excuse to take it off. The idea of meeting Lindsey bare chested prompted him to open the new stainless-steel fridge and pop the top on a beer.

He took care of the basics, securing the doors and windows, getting the bed ready, putting a pillow and blanket on the leather couch. All the while having no trouble picturing Lindsey's sun-kissed skin lathered in soap. And no problem imagining the small bubbles being rinsed away. Or how he wished he was in that shower with her.

"Damn it. Get a grip."

The water stopped and he reached for another beer.

"You look as if you've gone for a run," she said, stepping from the bathroom in a short, skimpy T-shirt and shorts cut up to her hips. Her hair was wrapped inside a stark-white towel that made her skin all the more appealing.

He gulped down the cool liquid, swallowing the desire building low in his belly. Any sweat on his upper lip was purely from his heavy breathing, not any labor he'd done while she was cooling off.

She crossed the small area rug in her bare feet, making him glad he was still in his boots. Maybe checking the perimeter one more time was a good idea. It would get him out of the house and out of arm's reach.

"How do we start looking for someone we know nothing about?"

"We know something about him." He tipped the end of his second beer between his lips and crushed the empty can before setting it on the table. "He can't fight worth a Hoover Dam."

"Well, neither can I." Lindsey unwrapped the towel and shook her hair down her back, finger combing and fluffing the damp wheat-colored strands. She dropped the towel over the chair next to him. "Seriously, where do we start?"

He had himself under control. Right up to when she batted those long lashes in his direction and those baby blues taunted him with their brilliance.

She took a step back and he caught her hand. With a little tug and footwork he remembered from the couple of times he'd danced in public, he had Lindsey securely wrapped in his arms. It might be very ungentlemanly, but he had every intention of kissing her until she admitted she wanted to see if the bed was as new as the kitchen appliances.

"How 'bout where we left off?" he whispered, almost afraid to ask. He had to ask, of course. Because as much as he wanted to show her she couldn't resist him, the decision had to be hers.

She didn't move, but she was far from frozen. With his free hand, he traced the outline of her mouth. She sighed as her lips parted and her eyes closed. Her head tilted to the perfect angle for him to enjoy his prize.

He expected something to happen. An interruption. Someone handing him his hat or waving from the porch.

But no one was there. They were alone. Far from his family or danger. No one would be stopping them but them.

He hesitated too long and she opened her soft, sexually charged eyes. Then she followed the path his finger had taken and moistened her lips. He was a goner. Had been the moment he'd sat at that table and finally spoken to her at the sandwich shop. His dad had told him more than once that when he fell, it would be hard, and there'd be no coming back.

He leaned closer, breathing the same breath she didn't seem able to catch. His hand skimmed her silky skin and continued down her back. Her curves met his chest with little resistance, just as her lips crushed into his. She might not realize that he'd fallen and couldn't come back. It might not be the time to tell her, but it was definitely the time to show her.

If he did it well enough, maybe she'd fall just as hard.

Chapter Sixteen

Staring at Brian's lips made Lindsey want to devour him like fresh water after hours in the surf. Tasting him? Wow. Just wow.

He sipped her like hot chocolate on the beach in front of a bonfire. She could hear the surf pounding between her ears, building. The crescendo had never felt so welcome or right.

Making love to Brian here, in a strange house owned by a man she'd never met, was a little more than crazy. But she kissed him back. Long and hard and enthusiastically.

They only made it a few steps away from the table. Her arms risked a journey to his back, pulling his work-hardened body closer. Anticipation pulsed through her with every gulping breath. She wanted to get the feel of cotton from under her fingers and leave nothing between them.

Kissing Brian took her to the top of the highest wave she'd ever ridden. She should rethink, slow them down. But just like being at the top of that magical crest, it was too late to turn back. The hard ridge against his zipper left no doubt where he thought they were headed.

He ran his tongue down her throat, nipping sensitive places along the way—places she had no idea existed.

It was as if they'd never been discovered before. She clamped her eyes shut as all the blood rushed from her brain and her knees.

Lindsey hadn't thought about the way she'd dressed until Brian's hands slipped higher under her shirt, brushing skin and nothing else. Her hands rose and slowed his advancing fingers. When she'd left the shower, she hadn't allowed herself to imagine being this close to Brian. She'd been ready to get started on their manhunt, not curl up next to him. When she lifted the pressure from his hands he'd find out just how ready she'd become. But he knew that. She could see it in the smoldering embers of his eyes.

Lindsey tugged the soft, worn shirt over her head and her damp hair swished against her blistering skin. Her arms came down on top of his shoulders. Before she could discover the sinewy lines of his muscles, his mouth captured one nipple while his fingers circled the other.

The instant his calloused palm brushed her, she wanted to scream for more. There was no way to stop the reaction building inside. She wanted to torture him by running her nails across his tanned muscles and teasing him into mindless oblivion.

Somewhere in her brain, some neurons fired a warning. Where they were exploring was dangerous waters. She'd never been the type to venture too deep without her surfboard. Even though she knew it could only end in disaster, she wanted him beyond reason.

A relationship with Brian would be like a tourist on a bodyboard preventing real surfers from enjoying the waves. Or worse, pearl diving off the front of her board on takeoff. Why would she set herself up for failure? She knew nothing about family, roots, ranches or animals. Her life had been waves, sand and sunsets.

Unfamiliar thoughts floated through her mind, mixing with the sexy essence of who Brian was. Someone she'd been attracted to from the first time she'd noticed him. It was one of the reasons she'd remembered him so clearly from the coffee shop. There was something familiar, something comfortable and something so sexy she couldn't think straight half the time she looked at him.

Her fingers reached for his belt buckle, big and all cowboyish. His mouth nipped her breast, causing a hitch in her breathing. She was used to drawstring swim trunks and baggy jeans, but she'd noticed Brian's tight jeans once or twice. Maybe three or four times if she was forced to admit the truth.

The way they hugged his thighs and backside. Just thinking about him made a shiver travel the length of her body. She had her fingers on his zipper when he twirled her around and wrapped his arms tight—one covered her breasts, the other kept her waist close to his rigid body.

"Are you sure you want to go there?" he whispered in her ear. His breath shot all sorts of tingles down her spine. "Once we reach the bedroom, I'm not sure I can turn back."

"Yes and yes again." The words were spoken without a thought to any of the concerns she'd had seconds ago. Her body was already humming for release. "Don't you want—"

"Definitely." His voice was deep, husky, sexy. He nipped on her neck to the soft flesh of her shoulder. The evidence of just how much he wanted to continue pressed against her as she squirmed in delight. His hands wandered over her aching flesh. "Walk."

"How can I when you're… Oh, my."

His fingertips dipped under the elastic of her shorts. Teasing her before pulling back. He swung her into his arms and carried her to the bedroom, dropping her on the bed.

"If we don't get naked fast, I'm going to make love to you with my boots on."

They laughed together, kissing and tugging at his clothes. He ripped his shirt off over his head, baring his strong shoulders, revealing a smattering of chest hair that made him even more sexy.

As much as she adored her cowboy/paramedic, she wanted to see all of him. She tugged at his jeans, lifting one leg into the air, reaching for his boot. He lost his balance and toppled next to her on the bed.

Brian smiled the most genuine grin she'd seen, lying nose to nose next to her. One of those moments she'd dreamed about imitating from a book or movie. A moment where grins and laughter turn into a monumental life-changing instant. Maybe the thought changed her expression, but in an instant, Brian's changed.

He reached out and cupped her cheek, turning to his side, close enough and suddenly so serious she wanted to remember every detail. This time was different. She felt it. Knew it.

At this exact moment in time…this was exactly where she was supposed to be. With this man who looked at her as though she was the only woman who could ever make him smile like that.

Later, she may get mad at herself for being irresponsible. But she had such a strong desire to be the only woman who would be in this position with him again. And that scared the daylights out of her.

Brian watched the laughter leave Lindsey's beautiful face. He almost jumped off the bed to save her the embarrassing trouble of talking her way out of his arms and back into her clothes. Then her lips parted, waiting for his kiss.

There was no mistaking the longing. He felt it in the depths of his soul.

Playfulness was replaced with frenzied touching and heavy caresses. They rolled, scooted, shifted to the middle of the king-size bed. Overkill for the room, but he didn't care and wasn't analyzing why Mac didn't want more than a bed in the bedroom.

He cupped a set of perfect breasts, dragging his thumbs across each, causing the perfect rose-colored peaks to tease him more. Lindsey tugged at his belt, not realizing the tip of her tongue was squeezed between her lips and driving him insane. She unbuttoned the top of his fly and he couldn't resist. He devoured every inch of her skin, shoving the short shorts down her hips as he discovered all her contours and secrets. He still couldn't believe she was his.

For one night or a single moment.

"You still have your boots on." She sighed, arching her back as his hand continued exploring.

Fortunately, he could toe his boots off and did so without much difficulty. His jeans were a different story. He might get them off if he stood, but there was no way he'd stop the passion that was building inside of Lindsey. And then there was the problem of preparedness. He hadn't exactly been thinking of casual sex, since he'd spent all his free time following Lindsey during the past two months.

So his pants would stay zipped and they'd be safe. But there was no reason Lindsey couldn't have some fun. He could see her getting closer and closer to fulfillment. She tipped her head back, surrounded by a halo of hair. Her body arched into his hand and relaxed, finally opening the eyes he loved to look into.

"I don't think this is at all fair." She paused, gesturing to his jeans. "You still have clothes on."

"And they're staying there." No condom. No sex.

"What?" Realization washed over her face. "Oh. I saw…" She shivered under his hand again and drew in a deep breath. "He has them on his…in his bathroom."

"Lindsey, we can't do—"

She sprung from the bed. "Get out of those jeans. No socks either." She ran from the room.

He didn't waste any time. He stood, stripped his jeans, boxers and socks and by the time he'd stopped dancing on one foot, she was waltzing back into the room, tearing a small package.

One look at him and she stopped in her tracks, taking a long stare at his splendid physique. A lesser man might have been intimidated. Hell, he might have been if she'd stayed in the doorway too much longer. When she leaped on him, he fell backward onto a soft mattress and he stopped wondering about everything.

With a hand on either side of his shoulders, Lindsey lifted herself open for a fun attack. He dropped light kisses across her clavicle, finding her pulse strong and rapid at the base of her throat. He skimmed his chin stubble across her smooth flesh, causing her to sit up.

She lightly raked her nails from his shoulder to his hip. He sucked air through his teeth as she shifted on his lap and rolled the condom into place. Brian ran his hands around her thighs to her bottom. He pulled her hips closer, using himself to excite her until she dropped her chest to his, catching her breath.

Panting, she took his face in her hands and kissed him deep and long. Her hair dropped around them and he splayed his fingers through the golden mass. It fell around their kiss, forming a small cocoon.

Shutting out the world.

He searched her sky-blue eyes, close enough to see the darker flecks and count the freckles adorning the tip of her nose. He wanted to believe he had an emotional handle on this ride.

If he was honest, he was barely hanging on to the words he wanted to say. He knew what type of person Lindsey was on paper. He knew what he thought she was like from what he'd seen in the past twenty-four hours. He just needed time.

Time to discover if she could feel the same way. Even if she couldn't, he'd fallen long and hard. He really hoped Lindsey wouldn't mind keeping a piece of his heart tucked somewhere safe.

Stopping his teasing, he flipped her onto her back and slid inside. They moved together, their bodies hitting a rhythm age-old but unique only to them. Sweet, tender, hard and sexy until she cried out and it echoed through the house. He followed with a sweet release he wanted to repeat. They kissed, sated and smiling. He rolled to lie by Lindsey's side, the breeze from the ceiling fan cooling the fine sheen of sweat making love to her had created.

Simply dragging her nails lightly back and forth across his abs created another burn that wouldn't be doused easily.

No more debate why Mac had gone with the large bed.

Chapter Seventeen

Lindsey was totally and completely exhausted. Brian was a marathon champion lover. Their schedule was completely off. She hadn't had four hours of straight sleep since leaving his ranch. They'd drift off, touch in the middle of the ginormous bed and wouldn't be able to stop the nuclear blast until they were both on their backs breathing hard to recover.

Exhausting, but wonderful. She'd never imagined spending every waking—and sleeping—moment with a man would be this rewarding.

"You know, we're going to have to trek back into the real world sometime soon." She pointed to the empty box of condoms that needed to be replaced. "The last two are on the nightstand."

"We've spent two days in bed. Searching, talking and—" he kissed her shoulder "—other things. It's time to make some decisions, Lindsey. We're even out of frozen food."

"I could always make a run to the store. I doubt anyone would recognize me and I hardly think you want to give delivery boys directions, as if anyone would deliver out here in the middle of nowhere to begin with." She popped the laptop open and read Jeremy's notes on the real estate book. It was what she'd been doing when

Brian had awakened and a simple kiss had led to a delectable round of lovemaking. But she was determined to find the reason Jeremy had been looking into the sale of mineral rights. It had to be a clue.

"You've been at that memory stick for two days. Making any headway?" He quirked his brows together, causing his crooked stiches to wrinkle. He was propped against the headboard, finishing off the orange juice they'd mixed up from frozen concentrate. "Mac's going to need his place back soon. We should probably think about our next move."

"I think we're close." She focused on the screen, hiding Brian's rippling muscles behind the lid. His simple movements made her want to close the laptop and continue hiding with him here in the cabin. No. They had to finish at least one conversation and make progress.

"You said that yesterday," Brian said from his side of the bed, swinging his legs over the edge and sitting.

"Well, it's true." She closed the lid and set the laptop aside, trying not to let her frustration show. "If we don't come up with something, then where do we stand? What do we do then?"

"Leave?" He stretched as he stood.

"The murderer is still out there and determined to kill me, Brian. Or kill the both of us now. You're the one who convinced me that running wasn't an option." She tossed the large pillows against the wall, then flipped the silky sheet aside. "Who'll run the ranch if you leave?"

This particular conversation would chase him from the room and she was going to follow him this time.

"Same people Dad sells it to next month."

They'd talked every minute they weren't making love or sleeping. She knew all about the ranch's financial problems and a little about how the town had treated him over the past twelve years. "Stop being a jerk. You told me you don't want him to sell."

She admired him for sticking it out, continuing to live there and help his dad. She even knew how Alicia had finally made him fight his twin so they'd start talking again. What he wouldn't admit was how much he loved working with horses. But she could tell. It was his life, his passion.

When he spoke about training a spirited animal, his face lit up. And she'd learned quickly if she wanted him excited to ask about how he'd improve or how to get a stronger breed. Then she'd watch the disappointment drain his energy when he remembered it was just a pipe dream.

"The bank will never give me a loan."

She rounded the bed and wrapped her arms around him, burying her face in his shoulder. "You don't know that, Brian. You haven't applied."

"I asked you to drop this subject the last time you brought it up, Lindsey." With the tip of his finger he drew a design on her skin, down her back, then back up, getting closer to her breast with each pass.

"Don't change the subject this time. This is important to you. Running away isn't a possibility."

"It may be necessary for you to stay alive. Are you saying you'd rather do it alone?"

"I'm not admitting defeat yet. I still want to find this guy." She lifted her face toward his, seeking a kiss.

He kissed her into silence and she let him. She was still tingling in all the right places from waking up in his arms. The desire to change his plan of attack and avoid this conversation just wasn't strong enough.

Making love to Brian Sloane was a pleasure she didn't want to give up.

BRIAN STOOD NAKED, drinking directly out of the carton of milk. The only light slicing through the darkness was from the open fridge door. It was a small pleasure, but one he'd enjoyed many times over the past two days.

"Tell me again why standing there like that makes you happy?" Lindsey had slipped into one of his T-shirts. The shirttail hit her low enough to make his wandering eye curious to see more—even when he'd seen more many times.

"It's simple. Because I can." He tipped the remainder of milk into his mouth, then wiped his mouth with the back of his hand. "I never get to do this. I live with too many people to walk around 'nekid as a jaybird.'"

Her arm circled his waist as she leaned past him for a bottle of water. Her soft breasts molded to him before she eased back to stand next to the counter. She crossed her arms and could barely drink through her smile.

"What's going on?"

"I think I've found it."

"A connection? Are you kidding?" He wanted to grab her around the waist and twirl her in celebration before she said anything else. Before they could discuss it further and realize there wasn't a connection at all.

But if he touched her, they'd end up back in bed. Two days of making love to her hadn't quieted the need even a little. So he stood here with a hand on his hip and an empty milk jug in the other.

"I wanted to know when Jeremy got curious about real estate, so I checked the actual downloads on his laptop. And that stupid memory stick that didn't have anything listed, but said it was full? I finally thought of the password to open the hidden files, and there are a ton of them. Copies of research and references to emails. An email that occurred after a string of conversations regarding mineral rights that weren't transferred with the sale of property about twenty years ago. The current property owner wanted to know if Jeremy would be interested in selling."

"Was he?"

"Jeremy didn't own them. They thought he was part of the corporation that does."

"How does this connect to a man trying to kill your family?" Brian searched the fridge for something to take his mind off the long and very sexy legs in front of him. If he attacked her right now in the middle of her discovery, he might not hear the end of it.

"The rights are worth a lot of money now. Jeremy was trying to determine which family member sold them to the corporation. He couldn't find any records."

"So you think the guy he was emailing decided to kill him?" He leaned an elbow on the top of the door.

"We could go see."

"Right. Just ring the doorbell and ask if this guy is trying to exterminate the Cook family?"

"Of course not. I haven't thought of everything." She smiled, taunting him by crossing her arms under her braless breasts and showing him the bottom half of her derriere as she spun around. "But I did think of something to pass the time until we have to leave."

It hit him. Just like that, he didn't want to leave. Didn't want her in danger. He tried to hold his finger off the panic button, but it wasn't working. He wanted her safe, wanted to turn the evidence over to the police and keep her hidden somewhere. He wanted to tell her he loved her.

Just like that. In an instant, he knew.

"Lindsey?" He took a step, spun her into his arms and let the fridge door shut. His eyes adjusted as he stared into hers, wanting to tell her. He couldn't wrap his mind around saying the three little words aloud. He'd never done it. Never expected that he ever would.

"What's the matter? You said we needed a game plan. The lady lives straight up Interstate 35."

"I wanted to…" After. He should tell her later. Somewhere romantic. Not naked as the day he was born in a kitchen. "Never mind. You said a woman?"

"I searched the map for her address. One of her emails said she divorced a second cousin of ours years ago. But his name is on your list of accidents."

"We should probably talk to her."

"You don't sound very excited."

Should he be? "I guess I didn't expect you to find anything."

"I would have found it sooner if I hadn't been so distracted by other things." She smiled, hiding a glance at his body.

"So there wasn't anything wrong with the…um…memory stick."

"Nothing that I found. Oh." The double entendre hit her and she blushed from head to toe.

"You surprised me, Lindsey." He reached out, trying to bring her into his arms.

"Wait. I thought you believed I could do this all along. If you didn't, then why did you take up for me in front of your brother? Was it just to score points or to get him out of the way?" She jerked her injured arm free from his hand. "Why did you bring me here?"

"There's a guy trying to kill you and—"

"And I was your alibi in case you couldn't avoid the police."

"No. I've been trying to help you."

"Right. And now that I have a real lead you don't want to." Lindsey tiptoed backward, facing him like a cornered she-cat, claws extended and ready to pounce to protect herself.

"A lead to what? Jeremy might have been helping a friend. Have you read all his emails?"

"I think you're wrong." She shook her head back and forth. "You have to be wrong. Doris Davis was married to one of our cousins and had nothing to do with Jeremy."

"Then why isn't she dead, too?"

Lindsey ran into the bathroom, slammed the door and turned the lock. He leaned against the door, wondering if he needed to coax his way inside. He heard a few words he assumed were surfer slang. Words like *feeling maytagged* and *launched from the nose of her board.* Stuff from a different world that he didn't understand. The shower started and then he heard tears. What did he know about those?

How could he apologize for making her cry? He didn't know what to apologize for, let alone understand half of the conversation that had just taken place in the kitchen.

He could be a jerk and ignore it. Pretend he didn't hear her crying. Repeating the conversation in his head, he could see that Lindsey might have been excited about her clue. It had just taken him by surprise. *So tell her!*

He knocked.

"Lindsey?"

"Go away. I don't need your help."

"Come on, now. Whatever you think you heard, I didn't mean it."

"Think I heard?"

The door flew open. His blue-eyed beauty was covered in soap bubbles—not far from what he'd imagined the first night here. The fire in her blood turned her eyes a deep sea blue. He hadn't seen them close to that color before.

One hand was on her perfect hip and the other on the door until she started wagging a finger at him. "What do you mean, think I heard? Because I know what tone I heard in your voice and I know what we've done for the past two days."

"I didn't bring you here to stay in bed."

"But we did. You didn't do anything to try to find the family connection to the murderer." She pushed his chest with her finger, slipping a little on the tiled floor.

He reached to steady her. She was as slippery as a newborn colt that didn't want to be handled. "You took me by surprise. That's all."

He'd been prepared for another round in bed, not a revelation that she'd found a connection that would put her in the murderer's path again.

"I think you wanted me to fail so you wouldn't have to help me. We could wait it out here until your brother's friends figured everything out and the police caught the guy."

"What's wrong with laying low and allowing someone with experience to help? It's better than spending the time in jail."

"You want to know what else I think? I think you *want* to run away from home. Away from all the problems you've been facing. Maybe someplace where you can be *nekid as a jaybird*." She impersonated his heavy Southern accent perfectly.

"If I'm such a jerk, maybe you shouldn't have anything to do with me." He released her and she skidded across the floor, catching herself before she fell.

"I don't think—"

"Wait. You got your turn to talk. Now it's mine." He didn't really want to say anything at all. But he didn't want to hear an explanation from her either. He'd claimed it was his turn and she was waiting on him. "I knocked on this door to apologize. For what, I didn't know, but I was going to do it. We just met and I get that. I understand where you might get the impression I wasn't enthusiastic about tracking a murderer. Go figure. I'm not thrilled about being a murder suspect—in your murder, no less. But you should probably rein it in a little before assuming you know what makes me tick. You don't have a damn clue."

He left her near the side of the tub, her eyebrows drawn together in confusion, but he didn't care. He didn't really know Lindsey Cook. He knew the woman he'd created in his head.

He was used to people assuming they knew what type of person he was. Used to people assuming the worst. Used to— He swallowed hard, pulling on his jeans. He was used to being alone.

Chapter Eighteen

"Where is she? Where can that little bitch be hiding?"

Pacing the length of his couch, he chided himself to hold his chatter to a minimum. And promptly reminded himself he hadn't switched on the recorder this evening. He'd decided against rambling and would record a summary of this segment of the chase after he was done.

Talking to himself had become a habit. Especially in his office. Frustration would make him look bad and he was never going to let anyone see him in this panicky state.

He'd been checking various places for two days. After the police had finished with an apartment in Fort Worth, he'd taken a visit to see if any clue as to their destination had been overlooked. But to his consternation, nothing. No one had returned to the apartment. Even the paramedics hadn't returned. Neither Brian Sloane nor Lindsey Cook had called or been to the ranch since he'd encountered them at Jeremy's home.

One delight, which shouldn't have surprised him, was the amount of information Brian had collected on the demise of the Cook family. Sloane had managed to discover all the victims, putting together cities and timelines. There were a lot of question marks in the margins of the murder articles. And someone had put together a family tree, including carefully printed death dates.

He'd placed the rendering safely with his other keepsakes.

He poured himself yet another vodka. He'd lost count how many he'd had since sending his secretary home for the night. The decanter was nearly empty. Frustration did that to him. It made him break his rules.

If the couple would run, there would be hours of searching and traveling. He had looked forward to this segment being over. It would take him a while to devise a new plan, find new victims, new rewards.

If they had run…

"*If* they had run. But that's just it, I don't believe they have."

The police, however, no longer thought Brian had murdered the prostitute. After assurances from John Sloane and his Marine Corps friend that Lindsey was very much alive, Brian was only wanted for questioning.

"That's it! How could I have forgotten the Marine? He provided them a place to stay hidden. A home or piece of property the police don't know about."

Staying in the area meant they'd be surfacing soon. He didn't have to look for their hiding place; they'd reveal themselves soon enough. Did they really think they could match wits with someone of his intellect?

"The thing about those who hide…they always come out to see if someone's still after them."

There was nothing pressing on his desk, just a bit of paperwork that he didn't need to file until the end of the month. Other than the day he'd closed for his trip to Cozumel, he hadn't taken a vacation in years. Closing again wouldn't draw special attention. Perhaps it was time to finish this game.

He filled his glass with the last of the fiery liquid from the decanter. "A toast. May the best hunter win."

Chapter Nineteen

Brian unfolded his tall frame, grabbed his hat and shut the door. He stood at the corner of the car, waiting on Lindsey to follow. The car would be hot and she already had a layer of itchy sweat accumulating on her skin. She opened the door and swung her legs to the gravel.

"You coming?" Brian asked, not hiding the impatience in his voice. He looked at his watch as if he had an appointment to keep.

Behind the wheel, he hadn't been relaxed. He'd rarely smiled. Shoot, he'd been more relaxed after being in a knife fight with a murderer. And as many times as they'd ridden in a car together, this was the first time he'd rudely listened to the radio instead of talking with her. Going so far as to turn it up when she tried to mention the emails.

Mrs. Doris Davis lived about an hour north of Mac's secluded house. A house that hadn't been as far out in the middle of nowhere as Lindsey had originally thought. The drive seemed to take five times longer since Brian wasn't communicating with her. He was polite enough, speaking when necessary. But things had changed between them.

It was as if he had no vested interest in her situation any longer. More like he was treating it as an obligation. It had only been two days with an amateur—her—

searching, but this was their only lead. Maybe not even that. Jeremy might have been curious about something he found while researching his family heritage. There was no way to be certain other than actually talking to this woman.

As excited as Lindsey was to be at Mrs. Davis's home, she was more devastated that things might be over with Brian. If she could just explain… Maybe tell him how much she was scared the connection wouldn't pan out. How frightened she was of facing a lifetime of running.

She'd messed up. He was right. She shouldn't have assumed anything about Brian's motives. With her limited people skills, it was easier to move to the next beach instead of working through problems with people she liked. And she really liked this man. In fact, she could just be falling in love for the first time in her life.

"Lindsey?" Brian stood in front of her, hand outstretched to help. His fingers clasped around hers and, simply put, she felt safe.

Two hours without him on her side and she wanted to cry. How could she figure all this mess out alone? *Stop!* She couldn't assume anything else. Right now, she was about to verify what type of clue she'd uncovered—useful or useless.

"I feel stupid because I never realized someone was killing off my family," she blurted, staring at the ground. "If you hadn't done the research and tried to warn me… What if we never find out who he is?"

Brian pulled her into his arms, burying her face in his shirt. "There's nothing you could have done to prevent any of it. No one caught on, Lindsey. People with a lot more experience than us labeled the deaths as accidents. Hell, I hardly believed it myself until we found that poor girl."

"If I had paid more attention, Jeremy might still be alive."

"Or you could be dead, too." He tipped her chin so she'd look at him. "You were right about me wanting to stay at Mac's. But you got the reason wrong. I don't want you to risk getting hurt or worse."

"We can go back. Let your brother's friends take care of the investigating."

The front door opened. "You two coming in or what?"

DORIS WAS THRILLED to receive guests. They arrived for morning tea, just as scheduled, and she had the service all set. A full English tea along with a variety of cookies. It seemed very out of place, but so did the frilly yellow house surrounded by prairie grass and cattle.

Tea wasn't really Lindsey's thing. It was something you ordered cold, with lots of ice at dinner. Hot, flavored with lemon or milk? She didn't know which would be better with the vanilla macaroons she'd fallen in love with.

Brian sat next to her on a tiny settee, leaning forward across his knees, sipping out of a delicate china cup. His tight jeans hugged the thigh muscles she'd run her hands along such a short time ago. And honestly, he looked very uncomfortable. As if he were sitting in on a tea party for a child.

Doris, a petite woman less than five feet tall, refused to talk about her ex-husband during tea. Brian sipped away, and with every question popped another cookie into his mouth, then gestured back to Lindsey.

"So how long have you two been a couple?" Doris asked from her window seat.

"Us?" Brian shook his head and waved in Lindsey's direction.

Leaning forward like he was, she couldn't give him a

stern look to stop evading conversation. If she was going to do all the talking, he could just live with her version of the story. "Brian followed me around like a puppy for months before he gathered the courage to ask me out."

The cowboy almost spit out his latest bite of cookie. He stuttered over the word *no* for several seconds before giving up. Good. He could choke a little more.

"Yes, the poor thing is so shy," Lindsey continued, gently patting him on the back. "You'll have to forgive him. Even now, you can see he's barely talking to you."

The man finally turned his head, wrinkled the new scar on his forehead and growled a little at her. Doris didn't catch it. The silver-haired matron seemed to be a little hard of hearing.

Doris put her cup on the rolling service tray. "That's okay, dear, my third husband was just like that. I love the strong, silent type. At least for a while."

Lindsey laughed along with her hostess. Brian choked a little more, quickly swallowing more of his tea.

"Now, you wanted to know about your distant cousin, which would have been my second husband, Joel. Quiet man and terribly boring. I was so surprised to hear about his sudden death. When was it? Almost twenty years ago?"

"Yes ma'am," Brian answered, then shot Lindsey another look.

"Horrid little man, really. He didn't leave me a thing in his will. Now, if you wanted to know about my side of the family, if they were related to me, they were wonderful people."

"Can you tell me—us—why Jeremy was so interested in Joel's will?" Lindsey asked.

"We only got into that a little. I had no idea your cousin had died, Lindsey. The emails and phone calls stopped and I thought he must have been one of those scammer people out fishing for information. That's why I insisted on meeting you in person. You just can't be too careful nowadays."

"Right," Lindsey agreed. "You never know if someone's going to lead a serial killer to your door or not."

On that-below-the-belt jab, Brian set his delicate teacup aside and stood. She knew he hadn't meant to speed up the killer's timetable. And she also knew that Brian was the reason she was alive. But she was a bit miffed at him and he deserved to feel a little uncomfortable.

"Do you need the facilities, dear?"

"No ma'am. I just…have a cramp." He halfheartedly rubbed at his thigh. "So what did Jeremy ask about?"

"Joel sold his family home when we married and moved in here. The house wasn't worth much, just an old building that the next owner was going to tear down. Thank goodness his mother wasn't alive to see that happen. Anyway, your cousin Jeremy wanted to know if I might have a copy of the deed. He mentioned something about a trust that was looking for heirs. He was particularly interested in the mineral rights."

Lindsey was ecstatic that she'd been right. So happy that she had a hard time concentrating on what Doris actually said next.

"I don't think your cousin could obtain copies of the sales if they were available. It gets a little confusing."

"That's a shame. Sorry we bothered you," Brian said quickly.

"Hold on, Mr. Sloane." Doris motioned for Brian to sit back down, which he did. "That's what started our conversations, but it's not what really caught Jeremy's interest."

Lindsey sat forward, almost even with Brian. She

wanted to jump up and down. Detective work was fun if you could forget about the murder portion. She wanted to hold Brian's hand again. Good news or bad, it would be better with him along for the ride.

"You might have noticed all the cattle wandering around here when I am far—" she waved at all her frills in the room "—from being a rancher. I lease my land. Lots of people do."

Lindsey was trying to be patient, but she didn't want a lesson about ranching. Brian's hand reached out to cover hers. Maybe she was showing a little more angst than she had thought. She laced her fingers through the strength he shared and stopped her toes from the rapid, nervous *tap tap tap.*

"I not only lease my grazing land, I lease my mineral rights. Did you know you can sell your mineral rights?"

Brian nodded yes but Lindsey was trying to string the information together. Joel. Property sales. Murders. Mineral rights. "This doesn't make sense. Why would anyone want to kill Jeremy over his house?"

"Jeremy was killed? The internet said he drowned in Cozumel."

"We should go." Brian stood and drew her to her feet. His eyes told her not to say anything else. She pushed him to the side; he hit the tea cart, scooting it inches but rattling the china.

"Doris, why is it interesting? I don't understand."

"Remember I told you Joel sold his mother's house? Well, there's no record of the mineral rights being sold prior. So who owns them now?"

"Let me guess, the house is right in the middle of the Barnett Shale."

"You'd be guessing correctly," Doris confirmed.

"I don't understand."

"Natural gas that's being extracted by fracking, dear."

"There's our motive," Brian cursed.

Something significant had just been revealed, and Lindsey was still confused.

"Thanks for your time. It was nice meeting you."

"You'll need the address." Doris handed him an envelope.

Brian ushered her outside and hustled her into the car.

"Why are we leaving? I had a ton of questions."

"We don't need to involve Doris. She's been safe so far. She needs to stay that way."

"Why wouldn't she be? And where are we going?"

"We need some answers."

"You're confusing me, because I thought we were getting answers back there with Doris."

"We need more information than Doris can provide."

"So we should have let Mac search Jeremy's computer to begin with."

He slowed at a four-way stop and instead of moving forward, he draped his arm over the backseat and got two bottles of water from the cooler, handing one to her.

"We don't need a hacker, at least not yet. Property owners are listed at the county tax office. We just need to fill out some forms. I went through that looking for the owner of Mrs. Cook's property. That's how I found the rest of your family."

"Won't the police arrest you if you show up at the county clerk's office?"

"Maybe. That's a risk I need to take. But just in case, I still have John's military ID." His smile was back.

Her confidence was returning by the minute. Brian would help her put an end to this madman's killing spree. Maybe somewhere along the way she'd find the courage to tell him how much she appreciated him saving her life.

Chapter Twenty

"Is this still a risk you're willing to take? Should we tell that to the judge?"

Lindsey laughed, smiled, seemed relieved and sort of drooped in her chair. She was handcuffed to the desk across the aisle from him and acting as if she was as carefree as a wild mustang. If Brian was jealous—there was no way he actually was—he might get the impression she was flirting with the officer assigned to wait with her.

It was almost an unnatural kind of fun drunk. Unnatural because he knew she hadn't been drinking. Yet her flushed cheeks and behavior suggested that she had been.

They were waiting to see if his fingerprints were in the system as John or Brian Sloane. They didn't believe he was John. They shouldn't believe he was John, but he wished they had.

Three hours had passed while they took their statements and waited for confirmation he wasn't John. He'd been very stupid about taking her to the county clerk's office, thinking no one would recognize him. The first person at the counter was very helpful and said she'd start looking for their request. Half an hour later he was under arrest.

What would happen to Lindsey when they put him in a cell? All he had was a working theory of why this serial killer wanted Lindsey dead. They had no hard proof. Who would believe them? Especially with Lindsey acting almost drunk.

"I can't believe they're arresting you for abducting me—a completely bogus charge," she directed at the officer sitting next to her. "Don't *I* have to press charges or something?"

She turned back to face him. He could tell her eyes were dilated and her speech was slurring a little. "I mean, I insisted on coming with you. And you weren't obstructing justice or fleeing a crime scene. You were protecting me. So how can they, you know, claim that you had anything to do with that girl's murder?"

Brian shot a stern look at Lindsey, attempting to communicate that she needed to be quiet. It didn't work.

"I can promise you—" she switched her attention back to the officer, but dropped her head toward Brian "—*he* didn't do it. He was with me the entire time. I mean, Brian was, 'cause that's John over there that you're trying to arrest."

She giggled and grabbed the officer's sleeve.

"Keep your hands to yourself, ma'am," the officer stated and pried her fingers free, allowing her hand to drop to the top of his desk. "Did this man give you anything? Have you been drinking?"

"Me? Just tea. Awful tea. Who puts milk in tea?" She tipped a water bottle upside down. "Empty."

Brian had heard that silly laughter before. When he'd gotten her half drunk before suturing her arm. He caught the officer's eye. "I think she needs more water or maybe coffee."

The officer shook his head, gave a disapproving look and walked into the hallway.

"What the hell happened?" he asked Lindsey, whose

head was sort of wobbling. She stared, her eyelids looking heavy and staying closed longer with each blink. He kicked the desk with his boot, causing a loud noise and drawing the attention of the officers in the hallway. "Come on, man. Can't you see something's wrong with her? Somebody slipped her something."

"Not here they didn't. Now shut up," the officer shouted as he left. "Your lawyer's here to pick her up."

Lindsey cradled her head in her arm, resting on the cop's desk. "I'm okay, Brian—I mean, J-John. Jus' really tire…"

"She's out. And you're headed to holding, Brian Sloane," a different officer said as he came over and began unlocking his cuffs from the desk."

"Seriously, man. There's something wrong with her. She has a cut on her arm. I haven't checked her today, but maybe she needs a doctor. Can you get her to a doctor?"

"There's something wrong, all right. You. Maybe when she sobers up she'll be pressing charges, too."

"You've got to believe me that she hasn't been drinking. There's something wrong and she needs your help." Brian got to his feet and had the overwhelming urge to use his elbow to knock the officer away from him. He'd been angry, but never over a woman.

"Nothing's going to happen to her in the middle of the squad room. I guarantee that."

Brian wanted to jerk away, wanted to run back to Lindsey. He watched her as far as he could strain his neck to see her. Once in the hall, he turned straight, catching the eye of a man who quickly looked down at his expensive shoes.

"You'll get your turn in a minute, counselor," the officer said as they passed him.

They rounded a corner. "Counselor?"

"Right. Your attorney saw the report that you'd been arrested and he's been hanging around waiting his turn."

It was on the tip of his tongue to state he hadn't asked for an attorney, but there was something about the guy. He couldn't remember ever seeing him before, but he'd helped a lot of people as a paramedic. Yeah, there was something about the way he'd avoided eye contact that set Brian's teeth on edge.

Brian was led to another small room. No one-way mirrors. Just a camera in the corner near the ceiling. He tugged at the cuffs out of frustration. It wasn't his first time in a police station. He'd fought hard to keep his job with as many times as he'd been hauled needlessly into jail.

There wasn't a way to shrug this arrest off. He'd be booked for dang certain. If that guy was a real lawyer, he had to make the cops understand just how much Lindsey was in danger.

He rested his head in his chained hands. The sense of utter failure hadn't hit him like this since the first time he'd been in jail for another crime he hadn't committed.

They'd been so close to finding this bastard. Twelve years of wondering why Mrs. Cook had tried to put out the fire and died. Twelve years of being isolated, never allowing anyone close because he didn't want to explain why his life was a mess. The first time he cared about a woman and he might lose her because of his stupid pride.

The door opened and the man from the hallway entered, carrying a briefcase that he set on the edge of the metal table. He took a step back into the corner. And if Brian hadn't already seen the camera pointed directly toward him, he might not have noticed that the man kept the top of his head available for the recording and nothing else.

The man shoved his hands into his pockets instead of introducing himself. Odd, but each thing built on the next and that fuzzy memory gnawed at him. Something about his body language. The way he stood, ready to pounce. And his eyes had a gleam as if daring him to…

It's the son of a bitch responsible for everything!

"Why are you here?" He knew he was right. Everything about the man told him he was.

The stranger's brows raised, inventorying Brian's position like a hunter ready to raise his bow. "So you've connected the dots. You are my most worthy opponent. I say that in all honesty."

"You don't have the right to say the word *honest*. You're a serial killer. A butcher. You slaughtered that woman for no other reason than she looked like Lindsey."

"You're slightly wrong there. I might have selected her because of your girlfriend, but I had such delightful fun. So there was definitely more than one reason."

Brian swallowed the rage building in him. Nothing good would come of him losing his ability to think. This murderer was baiting him. That was all. He had to see this through, get the man to reveal himself to the police.

"Guard?" Brian looked at the camera. Was anyone watching? Did anyone realize a serial killer was here impersonating a lawyer?

"Ah, yes. I realize you want me gone. I soon will be, I'm afraid. But not as soon as you'd hope. This isn't recorded." He pointed to the camera. "Privileged information and all that."

"What do you want?" he asked between gritted teeth. The muscles were tensing in his arms. He wanted his hands around this man's neck. It was the first time in his life he had considered seriously harming another human being.

"Why, Brian, I'm here to drop my gauntlet for a private battle."

"If I agreed, you'd have me at a disadvantage." Brian shook the metal, letting it make noise against the table. "Why the hell would I *battle* you anyway? You ran from our last fight."

"You did take me by surprise at Jeremy's. That won't happen again."

"Quit talking riddles and just say what you came to say." Brian laced his fingers. The small room was much hotter than where he'd left Lindsey. His skin seemed almost sunburned, a red haze almost. He was hot and mad at himself.

"I can see the wheels turning in your head, Brian Sloane. Don't be stupid. You can't cry out. No one will believe you anyway. I'm a respected lawyer who felt sorry for the way you've been treated throughout this terrible ordeal."

"It may take time, but the police can discover the truth. I know about your mineral rights trust."

He finally pulled a hand from his pocket, swiping at the corner of his eye as if he was laughing so hard he cried. "Oh, Brian. That's so funny. You've been accused of murder. Your DNA is at the scene and will match their samples. And of course, they'll find the knife you used on the prostitute in your barn."

Brian's hands were fisted; the metal rings pinched and scratched his wrists as he tugged and then tugged again. He knew he couldn't break them, but the gesture kept him from losing it completely.

"Not to mention the testimony of your lawyer when I attempted to get you to surrender after being interrupted at your prisoner's home." He laughed in a tenor old lady voice. "You're making this too easy. I thought you seemed the sort to fight. Are you, Brian? Are you willing to fight me and save the damsel in distress?"

Brian swallowed hard, keeping it together because of Lindsey. Wanting to tear this guy apart with every word from his mouth. "You know an awful lot about me. Aren't you going to introduce yourself?"

"In due time." He slipped his thumbnail in the small space between his two front teeth. "In due time."

"What's your definition of battle?" *You raving lunatic!* "And if you want to fight me again, you're going to have to get these charges dropped. Hey, you could do that, couldn't you? Confess to the murders and they'll let me go."

He nodded. "Right. And on a more realistic note, you know that the only leverage I have over your behavior is Lindsey? She's resting, by the way. I slipped a little mickey into her soda. So easy, no challenge at all. But you'd already guessed that, hadn't you?"

"Why are you telling me all this?" Brian could feel his chest rising and falling rapidly. His hands shook from the adrenaline. His eyes were slits because of the anger. He deliberately took a deep breath, trying to calm down. It wasn't working.

Nothing riled him and made him lose control, especially when he was aware of the situation and was debating with himself. He'd taken too many hits over the years and never swung back.

Teenagers, cops, drunks. They'd all hit him and he'd never taken a swing at anyone except his brother. It couldn't be the thought of Lindsey. In fact, his thoughts were different than the physical reaction his body was having.

"You drugged me."

"Yes, as a matter of fact. I gave you a natural something or other. Of course, I gave you much more than the vitamin store suggested. Are you feeling a little anxious? Is your chest getting tight?"

"You really are a freaking…madman." Hyperventilating. He closed his mouth, breathing through his nose, attempting to slow down the racing in his body. "Why are you…you trying to…"

"Trying to kill you? Why would you think that? You're the most fun I've had in two decades." He leaned forward to pop his briefcase open and pulled out a card. "You might go into cardiac arrest and these oafs might not be able to revive you. I would hate that. Such a disappointment since I'm looking forward to the climax of our story."

Even telling himself not to, Brian strained at his handcuffs without getting any closer to his target. At this rate he might break his wrists. His pulse pounded in his head, the veins in his arms popped to the surface, he felt his head rocking and couldn't stop.

The lawyer, murderer, serial killer leaned forward and slid the card down his shirt. The four corners made his skin itch on the way down.

"Don't disappoint me. You might have been clumsy enough to get caught, but I'm smart enough to get you free." He shut the briefcase. "That is, if you really want to end this venture and you're willing to do whatever it takes to save your little Lindsey."

Brian tried to call for help. It was a weak attempt. He swallowed air, not spit. Mouth too dry. Whatever this maniac had given him, it was fast and hitting all his senses. He finally croaked out, "Guard."

"We're finished for now. We should be able to tidy up loose ends soon. I'm ready to be done with this cat-and-mouse game and move on to something new."

The tightness this brute mentioned felt like a stampede on his torso. His jaw clenched tighter with each breath. The amount of restraint it took to keep from reaching up, grasping this killer's neck and snapping it…was only surpassed by the pain growing across his chest.

"You need to remember this, Brian. Do you think you can? Your car's waiting for you at the E.R. Clever of you to drive Mabel's. I'm going to collect Lindsey. I just happen to have a document assuring the court I'm her lawyer. I'll convince them I should take her to her doctor. I can be very persuasive. We'll be waiting. The card shows you where. Can you remember?" He tapped on the door. "Guard!"

Brian used his last bit of remaining strength to push forward, his hands jerking him to a stop inches above the table, he threw his shoulders from side to side, feeling as though he was about to explode. "You son of a… If you touch her…"

"Oh, I plan to, Brian. Many, many times."

Chapter Twenty-One

Every inch of him hurt. Brian had been thrown from plenty of horses. Had the breath knocked from his lungs more times than he could remember. Broken his collarbone and his tailbone, but he'd never hurt like this before. He ached all the way through and his fingers were crossed it wouldn't last long.

"Lindsey." He had work to do.

He was in the Denton Regional Medical Center emergency room. He recognized the sounds and the room even through his blurred vision. He'd dropped off his sister-in-law plenty of times. Why was he—? He lifted his arm…handcuffed and in a hospital gown. His foggy memory mixed bits and pieces of scenes flashing between shards of pain.

Lindsey. Jail. Drugged. Serial killer. Pain. Nothing.

Either all those jumbled memories had actually happened or he'd been kicked in the head by one of his horses and was having a very realistic dream. Yeah, it had all happened. He could remember the taste of Lindsey's skin, the face she'd made at the bitterness of Doris's tea. His days and nights with her were very vivid.

Alicia walked into the room, her finger across her lips to caution him from speaking. He caught a glimpse of a uniform at his door. "We came as soon as your story broke on the news. They said you began having seizures while at the jail. And we're both very lucky they haven't changed my ID yet. I doubt the police would let your sister-in-law check on you."

"God, please tell me you haven't seen me naked. And if you have, lie."

"Get a grip, brother-in-law. I see that exact body every day on John. But no, I just came on shift so I didn't see anything. John's in the parking lot." She pumped up the pressure cuff already on his arm, looking over her shoulder toward the door.

"Have you heard from Lindsey? That bastard's got her. I've got to get out of here. Fast." He tried to sit up, but his head swam, turning the rest of the room to a blur. The metal handcuffs banged. His sister-in-law shushed him.

"Hold on, buster, you aren't going anywhere. You're a very sick puppy."

"He drugged me."

"Are you stating or asking?" She flipped his chart to where he should have been able to read it. "They pumped your stomach. Juanita was on duty and called us when you were brought in. She said it was a little touch and go. Your heart nearly stopped, Brian."

The writing was blurry. He couldn't make out why they'd pumped him, but it explained why his voice sounded scratchy. "Alicia, get John in here. He's going to kill Lindsey."

"Are you still feverish? John's not killing anyone," she whispered, stuck a thermometer into his mouth and then wrote down his vitals.

"I'm dead serious, Alicia," he mumbled around the stick under his tongue. "I need John. The freak didn't tell me his name. He's a lawyer or faking at being a lawyer. But we found out he's working some kind of scam stealing mineral rights when properties are sold. He drugged our drinks in the middle of the freakin' squad room."

She removed the thermometer and disposed of the covering. "Calm down. You aren't making sense."

"Just call John. I need him to wait this one out for me."

"What are you suggesting? You know he's better trained to find this lawyer. Did you consider just telling him? You want him to go to jail for you?"

He tried not to be angry. He wanted to say the words that hung between them. *How many times had he gone to jail because John left and their small town blamed him for Mrs. Cook's death?* He didn't. They hung there until she pulled her cell, talked, hung up and then took his IV out.

"You're going to have a horrible headache. Can you even see straight?"

"Straight enough." He'd be lucky to see a hundred feet in front of the car, but he had no choice.

"I suppose you'll need my keys."

"Mabel's car is out there."

"How do you know? Oh, gosh, I don't want to know that answer, do I? How are you even going to find this killer if you don't know his name?"

Remember this, Brian. Can you remember? He'd put something scratchy down his shirt.

"Where's my stuff? I think he dropped a business card in my clothes." She shook his clothes. The T-shirt was ripped in half, his jeans looked just as bad. His Ropers were fine. He would take John's clothes, but he preferred his boots that molded to his feet instead of John's Justins.

Alicia tipped the second boot upside down and out fell a card.

"Victor D. Simmons, attorney at law. You didn't imagine him, but it doesn't mean he's a lunatic who poisoned you. It could have been that woman with the tea." She must have seen his confusion. "You called after leaving her house. John and I both tried to talk you out of going to the county clerk, but no, you had to rush in. You're as bad as your brother."

She straightened the room, putting his clothes back in a bag, stowing them, swiping at a tear and trying to hide a sniff from the tears.

"Hey." He bent his finger, gesturing for her to come back. "Sorry."

"Lauren misses you and your dad sends his love even though he's a stubborn Sloane man and just squeezed my shoulder." She smiled and her phone buzzed. "That's John. Pretend to be asleep when I leave. I'll get the officer to help me and John can get in here while he's away from the door."

She waved nervously and backed up, wheeling a crash cart behind her. She deliberately hit both sides of the cart on the frame. Brian closed his eyes when the uniform moved to hold the door open. "Thank you, Officer. Could I borrow you just a sec? The wheels on this thing… Don't worry about him. He's sound asleep, will be for hours. We had to sedate him."

The door swung gently shut. Behind his closed eyes, Brian saw his world spinning out of control. Alicia had been friends with him and John for a long time. She'd married his brother. He could forgive her for thinking he was crazy. The thing was, the jumbles in his brain had *him* thinking he was nuts.

"You were waiting outside?"

"You have to ask? Alicia filled me in. Why would a murderer risk walking into a police station and drug two people?" John asked, already working on picking the lock on the second handcuff. "It doesn't make sense, man. Then hand you his card? It has to be a fake card."

"Look him up. The cops seemed to think he was legit. He said he was my lawyer and waited until they verified who I was. I don't know how he convinced them to talk to me. Or how he could just walk out of there with Lindsey. It was as if he was waiting on us at the courthouse. He even told me Mabel's car had been moved here for my getaway."

"He drugged you so you'd be delivered to the E.R. instead of transferred to Arlington for questioning. Pretty smart."

"Smart or not, he's got Lindsey and I need out of here so I can find her."

"You going to be able to handle this? You were so out of it you didn't know I'd come into the room or hear Alicia fill me in." He finished and pulled his shirt over his head. "Are you even certain he has Lindsey?"

"If she's not at the ranch, then yes, I'm sure."

"Then find him before they lock me up, will ya?" John handed him his service weapon.

They switched clothes and John got on the gurney. "I hate to say this, but you're going to have to put a needle in my arm."

Brian found a clean IV needle in the drawer and stuck his brother's vein on the first try. He adjusted the IV to the slowest drip possible.

"You're pretty good at that. Ever think about becoming a doctor?" his brother asked.

"Not ever. I want to raise quarter horses." The response was instinctive, not thought about, not debated. He wanted the ranch.

"We have a lot to talk about when this is all over."

"Right. Now I need to concentrate on finding my girl."

"You know I'd go for you," he said, clapping a hand around his shoulder, smiling.

"I have to do this."

"That's what I thought. Do you know where to start?"

With a bandage over his forehead to cover the missing scar, the IV tape in exactly the same spot and handcuffed to the rail on either side of the bed, John looked exactly like Brian, with one exception—

"We forgot about the blasted hair. You cut yours."

"You should have cut yours. Hell, Brian, they won't notice with me just lying here. Alicia's going to check on me. The shift changed from when you were admitted. She'll cover. Just don't leave me hanging, bro. So again, do you have a clue where to find this guy?"

"The bastard said to remember. I can start with his flippin' business card." He looked on the reverse side. "Or follow the map he conveniently left with me."

LINDSEY HAD BEEN groggy for a long while. Sort of aware that she was moving and unable to react. Her eyes hadn't opened fully since giving her statement to the police in Denton. She remembered that. Remembered Brian and… confusion.

She'd lost control, feeling more like a lump of flesh being directed, molded and fixed in place. She couldn't see, barely could feel, but the fog was lifting.

How she'd gotten out of police custody wasn't clear. Neither was what happened to Brian. She didn't think he was with her. It didn't seem as if he was with her.

Blindfolded. That was why she couldn't see.

Someone was there; she'd heard the unidentified person breathing. The madman snickered a few feet in front of her. It had to be the man wanting to kill her. She didn't know how she'd ended up in the paws of the monster. But she was there.

A flapping noise—maybe startled birds flying away.

Wrists tied with plastic rings, she could feel the edges biting into her skin. Her arms were stretched forward, bent but not high above her head. Her feet seemed to be free. A smooth surface was at her left hip, something like a wall.

No one was coming to her rescue except her.

She slid her hands a little and a rope rubbed against her fingers. That was how her hands were extended in the air. A rope tied around the plastic. She took a small step. Could she shift enough to remove the blindfold? Maybe there was enough slack if she moved forward.

She screamed as her right foot stepped into nothingness and she fell. The rope jerked the plastic into the flesh of her wrists, halting her descent a split second later. Dangling like a fish on a line, she stopped kicking her legs and lifted her feet back to the beam where she'd stood before. At least she wasn't flaying around in midair.

A man's laughter. The monster was watching.

"What do you want? My hands are cut and tied. You can't possibly think this is going to look like an accident."

Was he having fun?

When he didn't answer, she strained, lifting her body weight until she could get both feet back on whatever she'd stood on before. Then she pulled on the taut rope, tugging until she was back where she started.

If there were birds… A beam, perhaps. An image of a high-rise under construction, workers walking on beams and steadying themselves on the beam above.

Was that where she was? High in the sky with no safety net? She didn't hear traffic. She heard nothing except her blood rushing, frightened, through her veins. Then the snickering of the murderer laughing at her.

She couldn't hang like this indefinitely.

With both her feet on the support—whatever it was— she held on for dear life and stretched her left toes until they pointed down. She had about six inches to stand on. What was at her hip? She gently kicked out, hitting something metal, a hollow sound like a chute of some sort.

"What do you want from me? Or from my family all these years?"

Even if she knew where she was or how to leave or any other small detail that may save her life, how could she get free? No, she was staying put, hands tied and already aching from pulling on the rope to keep her balance.

"Your Prince Charming will be here soon enough. That is, if he survived at all. Shame if he didn't, I was looking forward to our battle."

What was he talking about? Brian was in jail. She didn't remember leaving the police station. Didn't remember much after the initial interview at all. But they'd been in custody, she remembered that.

She also remembered the fright she'd felt at Jeremy's house. Face-to-face with the creature who had carved that woman's face off her. Then when she'd seen the knife coming toward her neck but slicing her arm.

The knowledge that she was on her own shot the same panic up her spine. She couldn't depend on anyone but herself. No one else knew she was here or knew she was even missing. She wasn't ready to die. She'd just found Brian and wasn't about to give up on him. Or her own abilities.

Her arms and legs shook, partly from the stress but also from the drugs. She was already weak, but had to get herself free. But how could she, with that maniac watching and laughing at her efforts?

She turned her head toward the creaking of old wood on metal. She hadn't heard him in a while, but she knew she wasn't alone.

Sunshine reflected off something. She could see it around the edges of the cloth tied over her eyes. She held tighter, scooted forward until she could lift her shoulders one at a time and inch the blindfold to hang around her neck.

Her first look made her dizzy, and not just because her eyes had been closed for so long. She was a heck of a long way up in the rafters of an abandoned building. Three long flights of stairs. Rusted beams, ducts and pipes crisscrossed around her. If she fell, she'd die from blunt-force trauma from everything she'd hit on the way down.

Heights normally didn't bother her. She'd been on waves taller than this. It must be the drugs still in her system, slowing her down and messing with her equilibrium.

With her arms in this position, it tugged at the stitches Brian had put in her arm. The strain from balancing and easing the pressure on her shoulders had started a definite trickle of sweat down her back. It felt like bugs crawling on her, which started her imagining all of the creatures that holed up in barns.

Including snakes. Hadn't Brian talked about barn snakes in the rafters? *Please, please, please...no snakes in these rafters.*

"It's very entertaining watching you discover your surroundings and trying to compensate. Good job, Lindsey."

"Is this some kind of test?"

"Oh, no. We're just having a little fun until Brian arrives." He returned to a post just above her where the stairs turned.

Logically, if this man killed her, he'd finish an objective and get away with it. No one knew who he was and wouldn't know as long as he kept his mouth shut.

"Brian was arrested. So unless you mixed up his fingerprints, you're wrong."

"My dear, I've gone to great lengths to assure he'd be here. So he'll be here. If he lives up to half my expectations, it'll be a worthy fight."

Had the other people he'd killed felt this way? Had he ignored them as insignificant? He'd been targeting her family members for at least twenty years. Why was Brian so important now?

"Did you kill Jeremy? Or my parents? Why? Why do you want the Cook family dead?"

"You want to alleviate your conscience? Make yourself feel better? Tell yourself that your cousin's death wasn't your fault?" He paced along a short wooden platform—it was the creaking she'd heard earlier. "That information isn't ready for public knowledge yet. Unfortunately, you won't be alive when it is."

"Can't you at least tell me why you want my family dead? Or even who you are? What did we ever do to you? And what does Brian have to do with it?" The sun was sinking, the shadows were getting longer. But she saw bright light from a porch or window. Someone was nearby, if only she could scream....

"Don't think about it, Lindsey." He leaned over the rail with a finger over his lips. "If—and I mean that in the slimmest way possible—*if* you manage to get their attention and they venture here to see why we're on the premises, I will be delighted to kill them, too. No thought or debate needed."

Dear God, what if a child wandered in here?

For all she knew, they were in a populated area and this man didn't look worried about being caught. Maybe he wasn't the one responsible for all the deaths after all? Maybe he worked with someone else and couldn't make the decisions on his own.

There had to be someone else involved. Someone had been following her. She couldn't recall ever having seen this man. Was he the butcher in black clothes who had tortured that poor girl? This well-spoken egomaniac was the same man who had nearly sliced her throat?

"Since I'm not the public and you assume I'll be dead when your statement's ready, it won't matter if I hear the imperfect version. Would it? I don't think you're the beast responsible for killing my family. You lack…authority."

He didn't like that at all. He ran down a flight of stairs until he was even with her, until he could look her in the eye and point his finger at her face.

"I am Victor D. Simmons. How did your arm heal after our encounter at your home? Or should I refer to it as Jeremy's home, since that's how you refer to it?"

"That proves nothing. The real murderer could have told you lots of details."

"You aren't going to goad me into admitting I'm the mastermind. I have nothing to prove to you."

"So you did kill him. You're the monster. A horrible little man who never fights face-to-face."

That got his attention. "What makes you assume that?"

"You cut me loose and I'll show you what happens when you give one of us a fighting chance."

He threw his head back in laughter, slowly clapping his hands. "Brava, Lindsey Cook. It's going to be thrilling to describe how you die."

Chapter Twenty-Two

There was only one place in Aubrey Victor D. Simmons could be referring to on his map. Brian knew the small town like the back of his hand. He'd avoided the main roads for several years when he'd been the focus of every questionable action that happened. Many years ago he'd learned the habits of the police and the sheriff—when they liked to eat, what streets they liked to drive looking for troublemakers and especially the speed traps on 377 where weekenders heading for the lake would forget to slow down.

That was exactly where he hoped both cops were tonight. Those heading up to the bigger lake, Texoma, would be heading home now. He took a slightly longer route, Sherman Drive from the hospital instead of the more traveled road. Speeding with blurred vision and taking risks he didn't ever consider while driving the ambulance, he actually made fairly good time.

Lindsey had to be in the abandoned peanut-drying plant that still sat on either side of the railroad. Rusty from top to bottom, it had been officially off-limits but just sitting there for a couple of decades. But every kid in town had played there sometime in their life. It was one of the few places he still remembered with fondness.

It was in the middle of town, across a gravel parking

lot from the fire department, which was next door to the police station. Brian couldn't just drive up to the front door and ask him to hand Lindsey over.

He also knew he couldn't involve the police if he wanted to keep the woman he'd fallen in love with alive. As his head cleared, he deciphered more of the jumbled visit with Victor D. Simmons.

The beautiful body he'd explored extensively meshed with the image of the woman slain in Jeremy's home. The words in that small room just before he'd passed out— *If you touch her... Oh, I plan to, Brian. Many, many times.*

She was alive.

She had to be alive. He wouldn't think of her vibrant personality any other way. Rage coursed through him with any thought of the lawyer's hands on her. Leftover effects from the drug that had been pumped from his stomach. He had to get himself under control and think clearly.

Running would clear his head. He parked the car two blocks from the building and ran, pushing through the aches and clearing the throbbing in his head. He avoided the police station, noting that no squad cars were there so that meant both were out on patrol, but Polly's car was in the lot so someone was manning the dispatch. He stopped at the corner where the city kept the fire truck, catching his breath.

Two peanut buildings—both were on his map. If he held someone captive, where would he do it? Hell, he didn't know and there was no way he could think the same way as this guy. He'd never have broken his opponent out of jail or been as bold as to face him in a police station.

Trying to understand a murder was not solving the problem. The only thing different about *this* Cook murder was him. It wasn't because he'd tried to think like a killer for the past couple of months. It was because he'd thought like himself. He was the difference.

He pulled the magazine from John's gun. Full, but that was it.

An all-volunteer squad meant the fire station was empty. He twisted the knob. Locked. He pushed up on a window and hit the jackpot. It was unlocked and he could get inside. He needed another weapon. A plan.

The way the adrenaline was still pumping through his system, it was hard not to rush in shooting and ask questions later. That was what John would do. He and his brother hadn't ever had the twin connection that people talk about. He'd accepted responsibility when he screwed up and John had sweet-talked his way out of more than one problem. Neither would work this time.

What he really needed was his brother and some of those SEALs he worked with. They'd have a lot of gadgets to locate Lindsey and extract her from a hostile environment. He should have swallowed his pride and just told John to take care of the rescue. But he hadn't, and he wasn't his brother.

Then why was he deliberating what his brother would do? The knowledge to save lives worked both ways. It was his grit that would find the way to get both him and Lindsey out of this alive.

And stop Victor D. Simmons forever.

LINDSEY WAS TIRED and drained. If she weren't perched on a six-inch beam three stories above the ground, she'd make fun of herself for being totally out of shape. It had been hours and several attempts to get herself untied, always resulting with a slip and jerking her arms from their sockets when she fell.

At the moment, exhaustion was her most immediate enemy. If she fell again, she wouldn't be able to lift herself back to the beam. She'd be useless if help arrived. *If help arrived.* At the moment she had her doubts.

Without any explanations or reason why he thought Brian would be arriving to honor him by "doing battle," her captor had stopped talking and disappeared. As if there was any honor in murder or abductions. Almost dozing, she wobbled on her perch.

Catching her balance, she looked again for a way to reach the knot. Her fingers were numb and raw from gripping the rope to stop the plastic from cutting her skin. She startled herself awake again, her hip hitting the chute next to her.

This time when she'd almost fallen, there hadn't been a snicker from some odd location in the building. Could she hope that he'd left her alone? Maybe she could get someone's attention if they passed by. But for as long as she'd been trapped in the rafters, she'd only heard a couple of children's voices, and that had been before night had fallen.

Groggy as she'd been, she had no idea how he'd gotten her onto this beam. And as weak as she was, she had no idea how she'd hold on to anything to get down if she could get free. The stitches pulled, her arms shook, everything ached, especially her neck.

A train whistle sounded in the distance. She heard the birds rustle. Then the familiar creak of wood. Her captor was on the platform. Somewhere to her right. Moving up or down or across, she didn't know.

"How long are you going to keep me here?"

"Long enough."

"Why haven't you just killed me?" her parched throat

hoarsely whispered, and didn't expect an answer. She'd asked before. "This is senseless."

"Nothing I do is without purpose."

Now she could see his outline in the dim light. The sound of the train grew louder.

"Ha. It's very easy for you to claim whatever you want since you refuse to explain."

"You're trying to taunt me, Lindsey? How very predictable."

"Oh, I'm not taunting. I think you're an idiot. There's no way that Brian Sloane is coming anywhere near this place. He's in jail by now. I'm just wondering how long I have to endure your threats."

"I think you understand that I don't threaten. I succeed."

"But at what?" She pushed the words out through her parched throat, loud enough to be heard over the train passing next to the building. A bit of dust falling from the ceiling caused her to shut her eyes.

Her captor appeared close to her at the rail, just to her left. Close, and yet not close enough to kick out and do damage.

"I set things in motion to make it impossible to say no. As predictable as human nature is, I'm confident he cares too much for you not to handle it himself."

"Flaw number one. Brian's smarter than that. His brother has kick-ass Marine and Navy SEAL buds. Why in the world wouldn't he let them tear this place apart and you along with it?"

The train passed the building, doing weird things with the light coming through the side panels that had broken free over the years. She tilted her head up. The monster looked even more frightening. Dressed in black again, his eyes loomed large in his shadowed face.

His fist pounded the metal pipe used as a rail. "He has to come."

"Flaw number two. I barely know this guy and our relationship hasn't been a piece of cake. Assuming he wants anything to do with me any longer is a huge assumption."

She didn't have to see his fist hit the panel of the chute that hung over his head. It shook next to her. Perhaps it was stable with birds resting on it, but along with the slam of his fist came loud creaking and a trail of dust from overhead.

"Flaw three. If—and that's a big if—someone decided to rescue me, why in the world would they meet you face-to-face for this 'battle,' as you put it? Even if you're honorable—" she tried not to choke using that word "—why do you think they are?"

"Shut up! I've planned this. My plans always work."

She'd finally gotten to him. Or maybe the wait had. Maybe he had his own doubts about whether anyone was coming. Whatever the reason, he raced up the stairs. Loose particles rained from the ceiling. She closed her eyes and dropped her chin to her chest.

When the train had passed and was somewhere in the distance, she could hear every creak and moan from the building. Including every wing flutter and scurry of small animals' nails clicking on the metal beams and pipes. The metal staircase and wooden platform creaked as they had every time the savage had approached.

She didn't want to look up, petrified she'd goaded him into action. Action might mean he finished her off. She ignored him, tired beyond reason and with no thought left other than keeping her balance.

More debris fell on her neck, sticking to the sweat, begging to be brushed aside. *Concentrate on your grip. One thing. Keep your head down and don't fall.*

A larger sting. More creaking. She didn't listen to herself, she opened her eyes, letting them adjust to the low light. In seconds she could see someone…

"Br—" *Brian,* she finished in her head, immediately stopping when she saw his finger across his lips.

How had he gotten free from the police? Why had he come for her? What difference did it make? He was there. She was free.

He held up a finger, then a palm. *One stop?* She shrugged, not understanding.

He moved two fingers pointing to the ground. *Walking?*

Pointed to his chest. *Him.*

Patted his back. *No!* She shook her head, silently screaming no. He couldn't leave her here. He just couldn't.

He held up four fingers and then pointed at her. He was coming back for her? She lost her footing with all the movement, one foot sliding off the side, and she wobbled. Brian was half over the pipe rail. She locked eyes with him, hoping that her fierce glare told him she was okay.

Her arms ached from the strain, but she managed to nod her head in the direction of the stairs. He stopped, one leg over the rail, ready to come to her rescue. She shook her head, this time agreeing he needed to take care of their tormentor first.

There was only one quick way down, and that wouldn't happen as long as the rope held. Freeing her was much more complicated than it looked. She was stabilized, and yet Brian wasn't moving away. She pulled herself upright, wanting to cry out, biting her lip so she wouldn't. Hoping beyond all reason the madman wasn't watching and ready to push her rescuer over the side.

She'd tapped into a strength she'd never realized she had and got her feet under her again. Brian waved, used his broken sign language to indicate he was coming for her now. She shook her head, mouthed "no," then, "I'm okay."

Tears of pain washed her eyes clean, but she was able to see the last sign he made for her. He stood with the rail between them again, put both hands together in the shape of a heart.

It was enough to make her lose it as she watched him climb the stairs. A heart. His? Hers? She waited, knowing this time she'd torn a muscle in her shoulder. The raw pain wasn't easing like it had before. She clung with her left hand to the rope and balanced on her right foot—her left ankle now caught between the beam and the metal chute.

She couldn't move and was completely helpless if the monster returned victorious.

Chapter Twenty-Three

Brian turned his back and climbed the stairs. He left her, obviously needing to be cut down and gotten to safety, one of the hardest things he'd ever done.

The noise of the train had covered his entry through the door. Overhearing the exchange between Simmons and Lindsey caused him to take the bottom three steps to intervene when the murderer lost it. But the knife had disappeared and Lindsey was no longer threatened, allowing Brian to press against the wall and hide. Simmons had returned to the roof where Brian had seen him keeping watch.

Leaving Lindsey now, dangerously hanging there, was tearing his guts out. It put another burr under his saddle as he took the steps two at a time.

It had been a long time since he'd climbed to the eagle's nest—what they'd called the east peanut elevator as kids. He rushed through to the outside, remembering that the stairs turned back over the roof. He could see Simmons ahead of him, dressed in black, but showing up against the rusted tin roof as plain as day.

Hang on, Lindsey.

Since Simmons was running, he probably knew Brian was chasing him. They both pulled on the handrail, taking the stairs. The place had been structurally sound sixteen years ago when he'd gotten caught exploring. Now he could feel the joints giving way, wondering if the rusted bolts would pop with the weight of two grown men.

He took the last step to the metal grating, did a one-eighty, grabbed the ladder rungs to the top. Just as he raised his eyes, his opponent stopped, and Victor's work boot caught him in the chin. He lost his grip, falling a couple of feet until he hooked his arm in the circular safety cage on the outside of the ladder.

Simmons couldn't come down the ladder with Brian blocking it. It was the only way down. If he descended on the outside, Brian could still grab him. He heard Simmons scrambling around the far side of the catwalk.

The blurred vision from knocking his head cleared a bit. Once he knew Simmons was headed across the chute to the roof, Brian bent and twisted to get upright again. He grabbed a rung, then a second until he pulled himself free to follow.

As Simmons jumped the rail to descend to the roof, Brian twisted through the safety rail and slid to the warm tin in time to grab the man's foot. Simmons kicked out. Brian avoided being hit by rolling to his side. He stopped and began racing up the steep slick metal. Brian caught the older man just as he straddled the building's ridge to head down the other side.

Simmons lifted his leg to strike out again, but Brian kept hold. Victor D. Simmons may have been older, but he gave as good as a weakened Brian. They rolled, and Simmons threw himself to the west side of the roof. Brian didn't let go and couldn't stop the headfirst slide.

Brian couldn't slow the three-story downward tumble on his own, but the hackberry branches helped.

"Grab hold!" He released Simmons and the man did

as directed. Brian grabbed a second branch before plummeting over the edge.

Why had he told the man what to do to save his hide? Simmons was able to sit, and began kicking at Brian's grip. Then he rolled to the roof joint, crawling over the edge before dropping to the lower side.

Brian caught his breath before following the maniac to the west-side ladder. Simmons was three or four seconds ahead of Brian, dropping to another peanut chute and running along the metal grate. Going up was the only way to get down. Brian didn't trust his swimming head or shaky hands to climb the pipe on the side of the ladder.

As he took the first step onto the grate, Brian remembered the gun tucked inside his waistband. He pulled and released the safety, but Simmons made it over the edge before he could fire. He dropped to the grate, looking for a shot, pulled the trigger, nothing. Pulled again, but he still couldn't hit Simmons mixed in with the crisscrossed metal supports.

Again, Brian was just slightly behind. He followed Simmons to the ground and ran as if he was racing from an explosion. Across the uneven dirt, back into the old building, swinging around the bottom of the stairs and each zigzag landing back up to Lindsey. He was within five feet of Simmons.

But seconds behind was all the bastard needed to lean over the rail, tug and then slice the rope.

"Lindsey!"

LINDSEY HAD PREPARED herself. If she fell, it meant her death. When the monster cut the rope, there was a moment of unadulterated panic. It was going to hurt. Her foot was caught and she'd be lucky if her ankle didn't snap.

There had been moments like that on a wave. She'd

known she was about to wipe out and the eternity clock began ticking. It only took thirty seconds to fall, but you can't scream underwater. Maybe that was why she was coherent enough to fall and stretch for something to grab with her good arm.

Her fingers grabbed the bottom of the platform where the monster now rolled in a struggle with Brian. She shifted, latching her hand in place where a board was missing. Then she became conscious of the pain in her ankle and screamed.

Hanging and watching the fight as if the men were defying gravity, Lindsey saw them roll and exchange punches. She clung tightly with one hand as the arm of her injured shoulder was useless. Still zip tied together, she couldn't get a better grip or reposition her good hand.

The psychopath scurried up the stairs, kicking at Brian, who followed. Then Brian fell hard onto the platform. The jolt caused Lindsey's grip to shake.

"Brian, the gun," she tried to warn. The weapon that had been tucked at the small of his back fell through the wooden slats. It clanged again and again as it hit metal on its journey to the floor she'd been staring at all afternoon.

Lindsey tried her best not to scream and distract her rescuer. But her foot was working free from her shoe. Once it was, all her weight would be hanging thanks to the loose grip she had on the edge of wood that was already cutting into her hand.

"Brian, I'm slipping."

The monster laughed as he stood on a step out of Brian's reach. Attached to his leg was a handgun. He unstrapped it and pointed it at Brian.

"Don't move, Brian," the lunatic commanded.

Her heel slid farther from her shoe. "Oh, God, please."

Brian turned on his side, his hand on hers. "Go ahead and shoot me, Simmons. I'm not going to let her fall."

"Uh, uh, uh. Not until I say go."

"If you wanted her dead, you would have killed her when you got here," Brian spat at him, but his fingers moved closer to her wrists and to the plastic tie.

"All right, hold on to her and pull her up."

Brian locked his hand on her wrist, her foot moved and she swung side to side in the air. Maybe the pain shooting throughout her body had short-circuited the neurons that needed to fire to scream. Or maybe it was the simple confidence that Brian wouldn't let her fall.

"You wanted to save her, so save her," Simmons demanded. "I'll watch you from here. I would like to inform you that I can officially declare myself the winner of our battle. It's time to finish this project."

"He's a monster."

"Forget him, Lindsey. Focus on me. Are you okay?"

"Just…peachy," she said through gritted teeth. "But I might…pass out."

"Come on, Lindsey. Stay with me."

Brute strength saved her. She could do nothing other than keep her eyes from completely shutting and passing out. She hung there as Brian lifted her like a free weight and saved her.

Maybe she did pass out for part of it as he pulled and tugged to get her through the rail. Lying on their backs, Brian clasped both her hands in his, bringing them to his chest. She didn't care how awkward or how much it tugged at the torn shoulder muscles, she needed his touch. Needed to know he was really next to her and she wasn't facing the rest of this night alone.

"Time to get up, lovebirds."

"I need a minute," Brian said, still breathing hard.

"It took you much longer to get here from the hospital, Brian. I'm afraid you got us off schedule."

"Schedule? You have a schedule to kill us?" she asked. She was too injured to stand and walk anywhere. Brian squeezed her hand.

"I didn't give you the impression that I'm a planner? Get up." His voice changed with the last command.

Brian stood, using the rail to help himself, then he helped her sit up.

"I said we're leaving. Get up, Lindsey." He kicked her thigh.

Brian turned on the monster, who acted more as though he welcomed another fight. He looked disappointed when Brian backed down.

"She can't walk on that ankle." He pulled his T-shirt off. "She has a dislocated shoulder that I'm going to stabilize. Unless you want her screaming in pain walking across Aubrey."

She'd had no idea they were back in Brian's hometown. All of the fighting and noise the two men had made and no one had called the police. They were still at the mercy of this madman.

"Cut her cuffs. I can't stabilize the shoulder with her wrists pressed together."

"Back up and hook your leg through the rail. I want to make certain you don't come at me."

Brian did what he said. The man pulled his knife and cut the plastic between her wrists. He put the knife away and Brian returned to her side.

Brian worked quickly. He didn't try to put her shoulder back in place. He angled her arm around her waist, ripped his shirt and tied her arm to her torso. He lifted her and took off down the stairs before Simmons realized he needed to keep up.

"Where are we going?" she asked, trying to use her good arm to hold around his neck and not doing a very good job. She rested her head on his shoulder. She was past any level of exhaustion she'd ever faced.

"Trust me, Lindsey," he whispered, then brushed her lips with his. He turned his head to speak to the monster. "Good question. Simmons, what now?"

"We need your car. Your story needs to come full circle for this town. Their hatred with you began during another *accident*. This one will validate all their fears."

She wanted to sleep, rest, not move. Every step jostled a part of her that ached.

"My ride's inside the firehouse."

"Convenient."

Brian had already been heading straight across the parking lot to the fire station. *Trust me, Lindsey.* He had a plan and he knew who this murderer was. Simmons. There were so many questions she wanted to ask. Brian's jaw muscles tightened along with all the muscles in his neck. He was either angry or very determined. Probably both.

Whatever Brian had planned, he didn't seem to like it.

"You're setting me up to take the fall for the Cook family killings?" Brian asked.

Where was everyone? It was just after dark and they were in the middle of town. She could see shadows of people from the lights behind the drawn curtains. Cars in the driveways. Flowers on the porch.

If she could see all that, what was stopping these neighbors from noticing a fight on a roof or the noise from the shouting? She raised her head, looking at the man Brian called Simmons.

Just a man. Not a monster or devil. A man who could

be defeated. She did trust Brian. They would find a way to escape.

"You really are an egotistical psychopath, holding me in a building down the street from the police station and a playground."

"And if you had called out to any of them, they'd all be dead. Keep that in mind, Lindsey. Just like now." He pointed the gun at Brian's head. "You call out. Someone gets curious. Someone else dies."

"Trust me," Brian whispered so softly she wondered if she actually heard him speak or if the words were echoing in her head. "Why come here, to town? Why risk being seen instead of going directly to where you're going to stage this last accident? Why the fight?"

"After our fight in Jeremy's home, you piqued my curious nature."

Brian spun to face the madman. "Curious about what?"

"Well, who was the better man, of course."

"I'm curious. Who are you?" she asked, looking over Brian's shoulder. She watched his eyes. Wild. Dark. Insane. There was no other explanation for his rash, odd behavior. Then again, was there ever a rational explanation for someone planning multiple murders?

"He didn't introduce himself? This is Victor D. Simmons, attorney at law."

"A lawyer who I bet works with people selling property and steals their mineral rights."

"I was right to assume that the two of you together would be my toughest challenge."

"My car's inside the fire station bay."

"Then we should get inside before we're seen."

"You'll have to open it, my hands are full." Brian stepped to the side, revealing the door.

Lindsey paid close attention to his brown eyes, wondering if he'd set some sort of trap inside. Simmons must have wondered the same thing. He tipped the gun back and forth like a wagging finger.

"Why don't you empty your hands and go through first, Brian."

"Okay." Brian kept one hand around her waist, letting her slide down his side a little, keeping her high enough that her feet didn't thump to the ground. He turned the knob and let the door swing open. "Nothing there... except maybe some field mice."

"Get inside." Simmons pulled the door shut behind him. "Where's your vehicle? I thought you said it was here."

Brian walked across the open floor toward the office, set her on her feet close to the wall and flipped a switch that turned on a row of lights with a high-pitched whine. "I lied."

"Stop," Simmons cried out, losing his composure. "We've already fought and I proved myself the better man."

The portion of the man who had screamed at her from the stairwell came into full focus. The man who totally lost it when someone said he was wrong. Brian was using it against him. But that man still had a gun and Brian had nothing but his hands.

Hands that saved lives.

"You see, I don't agree. You're not the better man at all, Victor 'D is for dumbass' Simmons. I think you're a coward. You can't call the peanut-dryer chase a real fight. I've had better fights with one of my horses."

Even in the dim light, she could see Simmons turning red. He was about to explode. Brian kept inching forward. His thumbs were hooked in his jeans and he didn't look as if he was about to fight with anyone. That casual, withdrawn voice was calming—no matter what antagonizing words were coming from his mouth.

Lindsey held her tongue, but while Simmons's focus was on Brian, she searched for a weapon. She quickly found the source of the whine.

They weren't weaponless after all. Brian had turned on the defibrillator.

Chapter Twenty-Four

When John had asked Brian if he could pull the trigger, he'd said yes. In his head and heart he knew if it came down to it, he could. But he'd had a crazy, wild thought while sitting in the police station—he didn't particularly like explaining himself over and over to the cops.

The empty firehouse reminded him it would be a lot easier to take Simmons alive and let him explain himself. So he'd gone into the abandoned peanut-dryer warehouse thinking he could capture a serial killer who had been at it for half of Brian's life.

Stupid. He'd stepped right in the middle of it. At least he'd had a backup plan.

Brian might not know a lot about how to extract a target, which was his brother's world. He did know a lot about what would take a man down without a weapon. And a defibrillator was perfect.

Now all he had to do was get Simmons near the paddles that had begun charging when he'd flipped the lights on. And he had to do it before he realized what the beeping noise behind them indicated.

"Are you a coward, Simmons?" He needed the gun put away, not fired.

"How dare you talk to me that way." Simmons looked

as if he was going to pop a gasket. He was agitated and his gun hand shook. "I have nothing else to prove."

"Don't you?" Lindsey asked. "You don't think I need to know why you were killing my family, but I'm the only one who can judge the real victor of the fight on the staircase. If you hadn't cut the rope, Brian would have won. So I think you cheated."

Victor Simmons laughed. His gun wrist went limp when he crossed his arms and relaxed. Brian hadn't expected that. A different man stood before them.

"Such a valiant effort deserves my appreciation, not my rage. I heard the defibrillator charging next to Lindsey. Did you really think you could manipulate me and shock me?"

Brian saw his chances of disarming Simmons waning. He began to charge when Simmons came to attention, pointing the gun at his chest.

"Far enough, boy. Don't you think I'm accomplished at the art of killing yet? It's been twenty years." He faced Lindsey. "You don't deserve to know anything. You're barely a footnote in my manuscript."

"Manuscript? You've written down how you killed my family? You really are a monster." Lindsey shuddered.

"Nothing personal, my dear. It must have been fate that brought your relative to my office. It began with a mistake. You see, mineral rights automatically sell with a property unless excluded in the contract. I made sure of that, but I didn't assign them to anyone. Joel Cook thought I was trying to cheat him and wanted my head. We exchanged words. Then blows. Unfortunately, he died. Purely an accident."

"There was nothing accidental in the other thirteen family members you killed."

"Oh, there have been more than thirteen."

One side of his mouth tilted in such a smirk, Brian itched to knock it from his face.

"I can see your anger building. You want to kill me for all the harm I've done."

Brian stretched his hands open, not allowing himself to keep his fingers balled into fists. He opened his palms, as if he was calling a stubborn horse. "That's not my decision, man."

"Where's your car?"

Keeping his back to Simmons, he walked to Lindsey's side. He didn't want to lose Lindsey before their relationship really began. This man would kill them both. He stood just in front of the defibrillator. It was charged and ready to go. All it needed was a patient.

In front of his chest, he motioned for Lindsey to grab the paddles and shock him. Simple. His heart would either go into AFib or stop. Either way, it would give her a chance to run. A chance to live.

She shook her head. He gave her a thumbs-up.

"Don't be stubborn, Brian. It's time to go," Simmons said.

Brian ignored him, counting down with his fingers: three, two, one.

He turned, screamed like a Highland warrior and leaped the last six feet before Simmons could pull the trigger. The gun flew from his hand. They both fell to the cement floor and rolled, only stopping because of the engine wheel.

Brian landed on top and got in the first punch. Simmons no longer had a smirk on his face to wipe off. He shoved hard with both hands, and Brian's shoulder and hand hit the engine. Hard. He thrust the pain aside and threw himself at the murderer.

Lindsey stood ready with the defibrillator paddles. Simmons was scrambling for the gun.

"Not so fast." Brian jerked on the man's pants cuffs, skidding him across the cement. He kicked out, keeping Brian a leg length away, then rolled and twisted to his feet.

Brian quickly followed. The man's eyes were narrow slits; he used the back of his hand to remove the blood dripping from the smirky tilt to his mouth.

"You want a rematch? Come on, boy. I'll teach you a thing or two." Simmons gestured for Brian to come at him. Taunting.

Brian normally didn't respond to taunts. He normally turned the other cheek and walked away because he was the one who always got thrown into lockup. He looked around the dimly lit firehouse. A place where he should have been able to volunteer and save lives.

But he couldn't volunteer in his hometown, helping the people who should have been his friends.

Because of this man. This man's plan to systematically kill off Lindsey's family had destroyed too many things...too many people.

His fingers curled into fists, but his center was ready to do serious battle. Just because he didn't seek fights didn't mean he was a pacifist or didn't know how to fight. He did. He and his twin had fought so much, his mother had enrolled them in tae kwon do.

His fists relaxed, he steadied his breathing, found his calm and waited for Simmons to advance.

"You think you can beat me?" Simmons danced from side to side in his work boots.

Brian watched for the first kick and deflected it with one of his own. He turned and kicked backward, connecting with the center of Simmons's chest. He absorbed some of the momentum when he took a few steps back.

Brian followed with two punches to the abdomen and then received a right cross that he had not seen coming. They both used trained punches and blocks, sending each of them into walls and the truck. Each time Brian thought he was getting Simmons close enough to Lindsey to jump stop his heart, the older man would kick or roll or throw a punch that could loosen teeth.

LINDSEY STOOD READY to blast Victor Simmons with a shock, hoping that she understood how to use the darn things. Braced against the wall, she'd loosened Brian's T-shirt so she could hold the paddles in her hands. She had to wait for the men to get close to her, unable to drag the machine away from the counter.

Brian was an excellent fighter. He could take a punch, but the way his body rippled was something to admire. If it weren't a life-and-death situation, she'd let him know how impressed she was. And she'd allow herself to be more excited about seeing his shirt off.

Each time the monster in black kicked or shoved or swung, Brian countered with a beautiful kick or punch of his own. She was so caught up in the actual fight, wanting Brian to knock this horrible person out for the count, that she almost forgot what she was holding.

Simmons crawled on his belly, trying to get to something. The gun. Should she drop the paddles and run to the other side of the garage for it? She couldn't run. Just balancing on her foot was too painful for words. Gripping the paddle with the hand of her torn shoulder was excruciating. She had to stay where she was and hope for the best.

The fight was slowing a bit, both men drawing longer breaths, both a little slower to get up. Brian threw a punch, pounding Simmons's inside thigh, and he gave a scream. Brian hit him time and time again. The psycho couldn't get his arms up to deflect or defend. Brian kept at him, backing him toward her. One last hard kick and Simmons went flying into the office door next to her.

"Are you okay?"

Brian winked at her. It was over.

Simmons lay on his back, crumpled and passed out.

"Get the gun. It's at the front of the engine by the door," she told him.

Brian turned to pick up the weapon. She turned to set hers down just as a bloodied hand grabbed her from behind. Simmons wrapped one paw around her chest. And held the knife to her throat, ready to slice her from ear to ear with one stroke. He used her body as a shield from the gun that Brian pointed in their direction.

"Put the gun down or you can say goodbye to her forever."

"Won't that mess up your accident plans, Victor?"

"I have contingencies." Simmons tugged on her neck a little. "I can still make this look as if you decided to kill her. That you abducted her and me and held us captive. Drop the gun."

Her eyes locked with Brian's. He looked as though he was apologizing. He couldn't do it. This devil couldn't win.

"He's not going to win." She didn't want Brian to surrender. He was the only hero in her life and she trusted him. She knew what she had to do.

"No!" Brian shouted.

Trusted that whatever happened, he'd save her.

Brian ran, the gun falling to his side.

"I trust you," she said, raising the paddles to Simmons' arms. She pushed the buttons that sent the electric shock jolting through both of their bodies.

Chapter Twenty-Five

Lindsey jerked and the paddles fell from her hands. Brian wished everything happened in slow motion, but it didn't.

He erupted forward as soon as he saw the look in her eyes. She'd placed both paddles directly on Simmons, but didn't she know the electric charge would travel through her, too? She had. *I trust you.* Dear God, to bring Simmons down, she'd shocked them both.

Lindsey trusted that Brian would bring her back from having her heart stopped. She crumpled to the floor, the murderer falling on top of her. Brian ran to the paramedic case and half dragged, half kicked it near the defibrillator.

Not so gently, he rolled Simmons off the bravest woman he'd ever known. The only woman he'd ever loved or wanted to love. The murderer had no pulse. Lindsey was facedown; there was a flutter, a chance. He'd told her he could keep her alive with a rig full of equipment. It was time to keep his promise.

The backboard was in place. He'd left it there, ready for Simmons. He skidded it next to Lindsey and gently turned her over to rest on it.

Training took over. He went through the steps that eight long years of practice had turned to muscle memory. Pulse. Breathing. Airway. Air bag. Monitor. AFib. Charge. Paddles. Jolt. Stop. Pray.

Pray harder, it's Lindsey.

Listen.

Give it a second. No more.

He was about to shock her heart another time when he detected a regular rhythm. Where was the phone? He searched the room perimeter. Nothing. He broke the window on the office door, grabbed the phone on the wall and dialed 911.

"Send emergency vehicles to Aubrey Fire Station. Police and ambulance."

"Please stay on the line, sir."

"Brian?" Lindsey called, her head twisting from side to side.

Brian dropped the phone, leaving the line open. He knelt between Lindsey and Simmons, attempting to block her view of the dead man. Taking her hand between his, he brought it to his lips, more grateful than he'd been since his dad's stroke that she was alive.

"I'm so…tired. Is he…?"

"Dead? Yes. You shouldn't talk. Just rest."

"Will they think we… That…I killed him?"

"He was a serial killer. We did what we had to do."

"You saved me." Her hand curved around his chin.

He caught it and kept it there, wanting to kiss her and tell her everything would be all right and she was perfect. But he didn't know if it would. Simmons was dead from the shock. Lindsey was still in danger.

"Shh, sweetie. I called for help. If I had the keys to this engine, I'd take you to the hospital myself."

"Selling Jeremy's house. Never step foot again. I want my beach. Don't you love beach?"

"I don't think there are too many horse ranches on the beach, hon."

"Nope. Not many boots…in sand. So sleepy."

"Lindsey, wake up, sweetheart. Stay with me." Brian patted her check and her blue, blue eyes opened, acknowledging him with a soft smile. "I hear the police, darlin'. Stay awake now, okay? Concentrate and promise me."

"I prom— Kiss me bye."

"Not bye."

He bent down and dropped his lips against her cool cheek. She turned her head, sealing their lips together. He wanted to devour her; the need hadn't gone away. If anything, it got stronger the more they went through. He straightened onto his knees again, hearing the squeal of tires on the pavement outside.

"Get away from her," Ronnie Dean shouted, pulling his handgun. "Cindy, I have two down," he spoke into his radio. "Confirm ambulance needed. Where the hell's the volunteer EMT?"

"Holy smokes, it's the fugitive, Brian Sloane," a second officer said, charging through the door. "What's he doing, trying to kill her?"

"Step back, Sloane."

The dialogue continued between the two officers who had pulled the Sunday night speed trap duty. He ignored them. The most inexperienced. The youngest.

Lindsey's eyes closed. Her head fell slack.

"Lindsey? Come on, hon." He shook her chest. "Wake up." He grabbed her wrist, her pulse was erratic. "No. No. No! I am not going to lose you."

The monitor showed her heart was AFib again.

"I told you to get away from her," the guy he didn't know shouted.

"Ronnie, you guys can shoot me and let her die. Or you can let me do my job and try to save her life."

Ronnie nodded and stuck his hand out to stop the other officer.

"She's in AFib. I need to get a regular beat back. Clear." Brian shocked Lindsey's heart a third time.

"But you're not a doctor. Should we let him do that?"

"Do you know how to work that machine?" Ronnie asked the younger man. "Go outside and call Cindy. Check on the ETA of the ambulance."

Lindsey had a regular heartbeat. Brian dropped his head to his knee, more than a little emotional and not wanting to lose it in front of these guys.

Once the younger cop was gone, he knelt to feel for a pulse on Simmons. "He's dead."

"Yeah, I know."

"How long until your rescue unit shows up?"

Ronnie shrugged, "Who is she?"

"Lindsey Cook."

"She's wanted for questioning. You kidnapped her?"

"No. He did." Brian nodded to Simmons's body.

"How do I know you didn't kill him, too?"

His beautiful, brave woman did.

"You don't. But you'll be the next one lying here if you try to move me before help arrives for this woman."

The younger cop came back inside. "About five minutes on the ambulance. What should we do?"

Brian listened to Lindsey's heart, now beating in a normal rhythm. Her chest rose with normal breaths.

"We're going to watch. If anything looks wrong, we'll take him down," Ronnie ordered.

They stared at him and he stared at Lindsey, willing her to beat the odds and survive. She had to live. They were a good team. She thought so, right? He stroked her hand and saw where the plastic cuffs had bit into her wrists. He dressed the gouges, biting back the emotion. Using the back side of his hand to indiscreetly wipe his eyes.

Then he secured her shoulder and strapped her to the

board for transport. He didn't want there to be any delay. It was a long way to Denton Regional.

The ambulance arrived, he gave them Lindsey's vitals and history, they loaded her and they were gone.

Brian didn't care what happened next. He was handcuffed and stuck inside a squad car while Ronnie argued with the Denton P.D. that had been patched through and wanted him transported ASAP.

Lindsey's care was out of his hands. If she forgave him for getting her captured by that monster, as she called him, he'd go anywhere and do anything she wanted.

Terror that she might die hit him. He couldn't hold back any longer. He dropped his head as low in the car as possible and let go. He kept the noise to some sniffs and a couple of deep breaths. If anyone had been watching him closely, they would have seen the tears of fright mixed in with the prayers.

Lindsey Cook wanted to go to the beach.

Brian Sloane would make sure it happened.

Just let her live.

Chapter Twenty-Six

Brian was asleep—or should have been—on the couch in his home. Or what would be his home for about six more weeks. Until the bank took possession of his family's ranch.

He'd showered and was glad to be clean, ready to smell like horses again. Even if it was only for a couple more days. He scratched his morning stubble and scrubbed his face, ending up on the new scar on his forehead. He hadn't received it fighting one of the worst serial killers in Texas history, but it would always remind him of finding one.

Brought home by a patrol car, he'd been released from jail in the middle of the night with the apologies of the P.D. No media frenzy. No reporter to tell the world he was innocent. No longer newsworthy. No longer employed as a Fort Worth paramedic. And no longer with a reason to follow Lindsey around night and day.

Except one.

He smelled toast, bacon and coffee. Time to get the day started. Time to face the family and tell them his decision. He heard the discussion and stayed quietly on the couch so he could listen. While in jail, no one had bothered to tell him why Simmons had killed the Cooks.

"The news said he wrote everything down," his sister-in-law explained. "In the beginning, he wanted the Cook family mineral rights. He faked their sale, was discovered and began killing. When he got away with it, he killed again. It became an obsession. The authorities said he enjoyed it and considered it a challenge to outsmart the police, so he began killing prostitutes. They aren't releasing how many died until they notify all the families."

"That was one sick SOB," his dad said. "If he confessed and they had a blasted book about it, we should sue someone for keeping Brian in jail almost a week."

"There wasn't a paper manuscript, JW. Simmons dictated tapes and hid them in a safe. So it took the police longer to sort through it all," Alicia explained patiently. "We're not going to sue anybody. We're darn lucky they didn't press charges against John for helping his brother escape from the hospital."

"Come on, Dad," John said. "We're burning daylight. Gotta get this place in shape for the appraiser if that financing is going to come through in time."

Financing?

"John, Dad, wait a sec," he called from the couch, looking long and hard at his boots. He'd miss them. His family and the boots, but he'd made a decision.

Alicia was drying her hands on a dish towel, John had just put his Navy SEAL ball cap on his head and his dad leaned lightly on the cane that was more for Mabel's peace of mind now than for real stability.

"What's up?" his brother asked, standing at his normal parade rest.

Brian leaned forward on his knees, tired when he shouldn't be after "resting" in jail for four days. "I need to say something, so don't interrupt. Got it?"

They all nodded their heads.

"First off, I'm sorry that I dragged you kicking and screaming into finding Lindsey and ultimately Simmons."

"Right, like we're going to be mad that you single-handedly stopped one of the worst if not *the* worst serial killer in history," Alicia said, putting the towel around her neck and leaning into John's side. "Right?"

"He said not to interrupt." John wasn't smiling, but he did drop his arm around his wife.

"We should apologize." His dad sat on the arm of his reading chair. "We could have been more supportive."

"That's not what this is about." He looked at his dad. "We've avoided talking about the ranch long enough. You're moving in with Mabel. Don't deny it, Dad. You practically have already. John and Alicia will have her properties to run. And I'm leaving. Well, there's no reason to refinance the ranch. I won't be here. I'm giving it up, heading to Florida with Lindsey. If she'll have me."

All three of them spoke at once. Irate, indignant, mad and just plain hurt. Then he realized there weren't just three people yelling at him, there were four.

Lindsey's sweet voice rose above the rest and asked from the kitchen, "What's he saying? I promise he told me he wanted the ranch."

"He told me the same thing the night in the hospital," John threw out.

"What are you doing here, Lindsey?" He stood, pulled her to him from behind his brother and kissed her as though he hadn't touched her in a year. "You still feeling okay?"

"I'm great. Are you? Okay, I mean?" His family had gotten strangely quiet. "I think we're all a little stunned by your announcement. I thought you wanted to be a rancher?"

"It's not that I don't. I—" He looked at his father and brother. "Any way we could get some privacy?"

"We all live here, bro."

He grabbed his boots and Lindsey's hand and pulled her through his family, straight out the back door with no explanation. His brother's laughter didn't slow him down.

"Hey, cowboy. Take it easy, my ankle's still swollen."

Taking the gravel in his stocking feet wouldn't have put a hiccup in his pace, but Lindsey reminding him she'd been severely injured recently changed his mind. He swung the best thing in his life into his arms and proceeded straight to the barn, where he set her on some feed bags. Once inside, he shut and bolted the door.

"Wow, it's dark in here."

He sat and pulled his boots on, letting his eyes adjust, watching her shy away from the horse stall. She watched for critters that might be near her feet. What was he thinking? She hated this place. She wanted to live at the beach, not in an old house falling down around his ears. But he had to explain, had to tell her.

"Don't get comfortable. Follow me." He led the way to the hayloft and opened the east doors, sitting down and dropping his legs over the side. The sun was just peeking over the treetops of the oaks that lined the drive to their house.

"It sure is pretty here."

"I love watching the sunrise from up here. Some mornings, especially the first week Dad was home after his stroke, it was pretty much the only pleasure I got during the day. I love the smell of hay, working with my hands, the feeling of success when one of the mares foals."

"I'm not sure I know one end of a horse from another. And I'm hopeless where cats are concerned. They don't like me and hiss all the time."

"It means something to me that this place has been in my family for over a hundred years. I was looking forward to setting things right, getting it back on its feet."

"What's stopping you? Money? Because I think we have someone willing to refinance the place." She paced behind him while he tried to understand.

Did that mean she planned on staying here? He craned his neck to watch her as she told him her plans.

"You see, once my financial stuff is settled—like selling Jeremy's house—we can get a loan in our names. What's that look for? If it's not money, then what's making you leave?"

"You."

"Me?" She sat next to him, dangling her boots over the edge next to his.

"Those are Justins. And they're extremely pink."

"Aren't they great? If you'd told me they came in this color, we would have bought some the first day. I needed some stuff and couldn't go back to…you know…" She pressed her lips together and shrugged. "So Alicia and I went shopping."

"You bought boots?"

"Of course I did. If I'm going to live on a ranch, I need boots to walk around in the mud and other stuff. Don't I?"

"I don't think those are mud boots." He shook his head at her expression, thinking he was crazy. "Lindsey, you love the ocean. You said you wanted sand between your toes. I planned to move because you wanted to live on the beach."

"Brian Sloane, it's you that I've been looking for. I was looking for someone to fall in love with. Not a wave. Not a job. Not a lifestyle. Even though I'm scared to death of snakes and I don't think I'll ever learn which ones won't eat me. Don't laugh at me."

"Come here." He was laughing and smiling so much it hurt. He maneuvered them back into the loft and onto the hay. "Did you just propose to me?"

"I don't recall the words *will you marry me* coming from my lips."

Their greeting kiss had been in front of his family. Not this one. It was a reunion. He tugged her to mold their bodies together. There was no doubt how much he'd missed her. She gave as good as he did and after five minutes there was no doubt how much she'd missed him.

He sat her on an old apple crate that had been there since the time of his grandfather—but maintained by him as a thinking stool. His answer didn't take much pondering. He'd probably made up his mind about Lindsey before he'd ever met her.

"I think I will."

"Will what?" she asked, the sunshine creating a halo of light behind her.

"Now that you've asked politely, I'll marry you."

"Oh, you. Stop fooling around." She threw a handful of hay at him. "I love you, but I refuse to say yes before we have an official date."

"What did you say?"

"That I want a date first?"

"No, ma'am. You said you love me, and that's a real good thing, 'cause you're the only woman I've ever wanted to say this to."

He pulled her into his arms. Sunbeams were flooding the old hayloft, and her eyes were the perfect color of blue that matched the sky behind her.

"Uncle Brian," came a young singsong voice from the yard below.

"Yeah?"

"Pawpaw wants to know if you asked her yet. And said to tell you to hurry up 'cause we want pancakes."

"Skedaddle, baby girl." He plucked some straw from Lindsey's golden hair as his niece left the barn. "Living here's going to be an adventure every day."

"I believe it."

"I love your boots." He kissed one of the bruises on her cheek from their previous *adventure*.

"They say with the right pair of shoes, a girl can do anything." Lindsey dragged a finger across the pulse point in his throat. "If she's lucky, she might even catch a handsome cowboy/paramedic turned detective/ bodyguard."

"I'm done with all those jobs. I only have one now. Loving you. That's it."

"I'll take it and love you right back."

* * * * *

COMING NEXT MONTH FROM

HARLEQUIN®

INTRIGUE®

Available June 17, 2014

#1503 WEDDING AT CARDWELL RANCH
Cardwell Cousins • by B.J. Daniels
Someone is hell-bent on making Allie Taylor think she's losing her mind. Allie's past has stalked her to Cardwell Ranch, and not even Jackson Cardwell may be able to save her from a killer with a chilling agenda.

#1504 HARD RIDE TO DRY GULCH
Big "D" Dads: The Daltons • by Joanna Wayne
Faith Ashburn turns to sexy detective Travis Dalton to find and save her missing son. In the process, will Travis lose his heart and find a family?

#1505 UNDERCOVER WARRIOR
Copper Canyon • by Aimée Thurlo
Was Agent Kyle Goodluck's last undercover assignment too close to home for comfort? Now Kyle's only hope to prevent an attack that would rock the entire nation is the mysterious woman he's just rescued from terrorist Erin Barrett.

#1506 EXPLOSIVE ENGAGEMENT
Shotgun Weddings • by Lisa Childs
Stacy Kozminski and Logan Payne must fake an engagement to survive. But with someone trying to kill them with bullets and bombs, they may never make it to the altar.

#1507 STRANDED
The Rescuers • by Alice Sharpe
When detective Alex Foster returns from the dead, he wants two things: his estranged, pregnant wife, Jessica, to love him, and to capture the man who wants them both dead....

#1508 SANCTUARY IN CHEF VOLEUR
The Delancey Dynasty • by Mallory Kane
Hannah Martin flees to New Orleans looking for help from PI Mack Griffin. It doesn't take him long to appreciate Hannah's courage and resourcefulness, or to realize that he may end up needing protection, too—from his feelings for her. _____

YOU CAN FIND MORE INFORMATION ON UPCOMING HARLEQUIN® TITLES,
FREE EXCERPTS AND MORE AT WWW.HARLEQUIN.COM.

HICNM06

REQUEST YOUR FREE BOOKS!
2 FREE NOVELS PLUS 2 FREE GIFTS!

HARLEQUIN®

INTRIGUE®

BREATHTAKING ROMANTIC SUSPENSE

YES! Please send me 2 FREE Harlequin Intrigue® novels and my 2 FREE gifts (gifts are worth about $10). After receiving them, if I don't wish to receive any more books, I can return the shipping statement marked "cancel." If I don't cancel, I will receive 6 brand-new novels every month and be billed just $4.74 per book in the U.S. or $5.24 per book in Canada. That's a savings of at least 14% off the cover price! It's quite a bargain! Shipping and handling is just 50¢ per book in the U.S. and 75¢ per book in Canada.* I understand that accepting the 2 free books and gifts places me under no obligation to buy anything. I can always return a shipment and cancel at any time. Even if I never buy another book, the two free books and gifts are mine to keep forever.

182/382 HDN F42N

Name _____ (PLEASE PRINT)

Address _____ Apt. #

City _____ State/Prov. _____ Zip/Postal Code

Signature (if under 18, a parent or guardian must sign)

Mail to the **Harlequin® Reader Service:**
IN U.S.A.: P.O. Box 1867, Buffalo, NY 14240-1867
IN CANADA: P.O. Box 609, Fort Erie, Ontario L2A 5X3

**Are you a subscriber to Harlequin Intrigue books
and want to receive the larger-print edition?
Call 1-800-873-8635 or visit www.ReaderService.com.**

* Terms and prices subject to change without notice. Prices do not include applicable taxes. Sales tax applicable in N.Y. Canadian residents will be charged applicable taxes. Offer not valid in Quebec. This offer is limited to one order per household. Not valid for current subscribers to Harlequin Intrigue books. All orders subject to credit approval. Credit or debit balances in a customer's account(s) may be offset by any other outstanding balance owed by or to the customer. Please allow 4 to 6 weeks for delivery. Offer available while quantities last.

Your Privacy—The Harlequin® Reader Service is committed to protecting your privacy. Our Privacy Policy is available online at www.ReaderService.com or upon request from the Harlequin Reader Service.

We make a portion of our mailing list available to reputable third parties that offer products we believe may interest you. If you prefer that we not exchange your name with third parties, or if you wish to clarify or modify your communication preferences, please visit us at www.ReaderService.com/consumerchoice or write to us at Harlequin Reader Service Preference Service, P.O. Box 9062, Buffalo, NY 14269. Include your complete name and address.

HI13R

"I'm afraid to ask what you just said to your horse," Jackson joke
as he moved closer. Her horse had wandered over to some tall gra
away from the others.

"Just thanking him for not bucking me off," she admitted shyly.

"Probably a good idea, but your horse is a she. A mare."

"Oh, hopefully she wasn't insulted." Allie actually smiled. T
afternoon sun lit her face along with the smile.

He felt his heart do a loop-de-loop. He tried to rein it back in as I
looked into her eyes. That tantalizing green was deep and dark, invitin
and yet he knew a man could drown in those eyes.

Suddenly, Allie's horse shied. In the next second it took off as if
had been shot from a cannon. To her credit, she hadn't let go of her rein
but she grabbed the saddle horn and let out a cry as the mare raced o
of the meadow headed for the road.

Jackson spurred his horse and raced after her. He could hear th
startled cries of the others behind him. He'd been riding since he was
boy, so he knew how to handle his horse. But Allie, he could see, wa
having trouble staying in the saddle with her horse at a full gallop.

He pushed his horse harder and managed to catch her, ridin
alongside until he could reach over and grab her reins. The horse
lunged along for a moment. Next to him Allie started to fall. He grabbe
for her, pulling her from her saddle and into his arms as he released he

ins and brought his own horse up short.

Allie slid down his horse to the ground. He dismounted and dropped eside her. "Are you all right?"

"I think so. What happened?"

He didn't know. One minute her horse was munching on grass, the ext it had taken off like a shot.

Allie had no idea why the horse had reacted like that. She hated that ne was the one who'd upset everyone.

"Are you sure you didn't spur your horse?" Natalie asked, still upset.

"She isn't wearing spurs," Ford pointed out.

"Maybe a bee stung your horse," Natalie suggested.

Dana felt bad. "I wanted your first horseback-riding experience to be pleasant one," she lamented.

"It was. It is," Allie reassured her, although in truth, she wasn't ooking forward to getting back on the horse. But she knew she had to or Natalie's sake. The kids had been scared enough as it was.

Dana had spread out the lunch on a large blanket with the kids all elping when Jackson rode up, trailing her horse. The mare looked calm ow, but Allie wasn't sure she would ever trust it again.

Jackson met her gaze as he dismounted. Dana was already on her eet, heading for him. Allie left the kids to join them.

"What is it?" Dana asked, keeping her voice down.

Jackson looked to Allie as if he didn't want to say in front of her.

"Did I do something to the horse to make her do that?" she asked, earing that she had.

His expression softened as he shook his head. "You didn't do nything." He looked at Dana. "Someone shot the mare."

Someone is hell-bent on making Allie Taylor think she's losing her mind. Jackson's determined to unmask the perp. Can he guard the widowed wedding planner and her little girl from a killer with a chilling agenda?

Find out what happens next in
WEDDING AT CARDWELL RANCH
by New York Times bestselling author B.J. Daniels, available July 2014, only from Harlequin® Intrigue®.

INTRIGUE

A DEDICATED COP VOWS TO FIND THE MISSING SON OF A HAUNTING BEAUTY IN THE THIRD STORY IN JOANNA WAYNE'S BLOCKBUSTER *BIG "D" DADS* MINISERIES

Dallas homicide detective Travis Dalton came to the city's seediest nightspot to put a deadly criminal mastermind out of business. Instead, he ends up rescuing a woman with haunting eyes he can't forget. But Faith Ashburn isn't what she seems. Her teenage son is missing. And that's just the tip of the iceberg.

For six months, Faith has been searching for her special-needs boy, only to discover he was concealing secrets that could get them both killed. In desperation, she turns to the rugged cowboy cop, who may know more than he's letting on. While she's in Travis's unofficial custody at his family ranch, he vows to protect her, even as the evidence against her son mounts. Now Faith has no choice but to trust this dangerously arousing man who makes her believe in a future she might not live to see....

HARD RIDE TO DRY GULCH

BY JOANNA WAYNE

Only from Harlequin® Intrigue®.
Available July 2014 wherever books and ebooks are sold.

HARLEQUIN®
INTRIGUE®

WILL LOVING HER MEAN LEAVING HER?

Bodyguard Logan Payne wants justice for his father's murder. Stacy Kozminski, a gutsy (and gorgeous) jewelry designer, wants revenge for her father's imprisonment. Drawn together by the circumstances and sorrows of their past, they stage an engagement while seeking the truth about their fathers. No one—including Stacy's own thieving brothers—can escape Logan's scrutiny as he tries to protect her from bombs and bullets. But in their pursuit of a killer, Stacy and Logan realize that perhaps their greatest risk comes in loving each other.

EXPLOSIVE ENGAGEMENT
BY LISA CHILDS

Only from Harlequin® Intrigue®.
Available July 2014 wherever books and ebooks are sold.

HI697